STORM WARRIORS

STORM
WARRIORS

ELISA CARBONE

A DELL YEARLING BOOK

35 Years of Exceptional Reading

Dell Yearling Books
Established 1966

Published by
Dell Yearling
an imprint of
Random House Children's Books
a division of Random House, Inc.
1540 Broadway
New York, New York 10036

Text and illustrations copyright © 2001 by Elisa Carbone
Map copyright © 2001 by Peter Siu

Visit us on the Web! www.randomhouse.com/kids

Educators and librarians, for a variety of teaching tools, visit us at
www.randomhouse.com/teachers

ISBN: 0-440-41879-8

Reprinted by arrangement with Alfred A. Knopf, a division of Random House, Inc.

Printed in the United States of America
November 2002
10 9 8 7 6 5 4 3 2 1

OPM

This book is dedicated to the Pea Island Surfmen
who rescued the passengers and crew of the
E. S. *Newman* on October 11, 1896:

Keeper Richard Etheridge

Surfman No. 1   Benjamin Bowser

Surfman No. 2   Lewis Wescott

Surfman No. 3   Dorman Pugh

Surfman No. 4   Theodore Meekins

Surfman No. 5   Stanley Wise

Surfman No. 6   William Irving

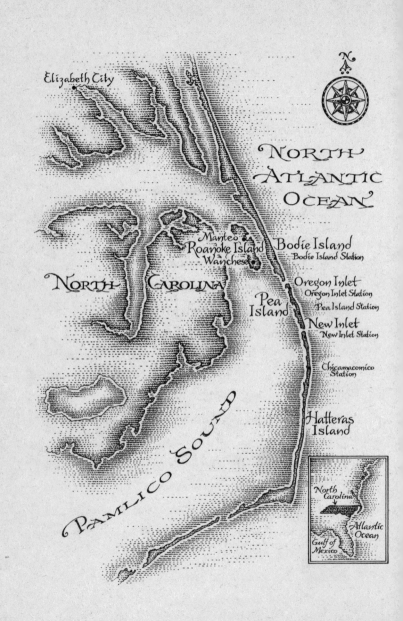

ONE

It's things we ran away from that got us here, and now there's no place farther out to run except the wide, rolling Atlantic Ocean.

December 27, 1895

Dripping. That's what got my attention first. Cold water dripping right on my face while I was trying to sleep, two nights after Christmas and just four days after Grandpa and I had climbed up on the roof and done what we'd thought was a good patching job. Dripping, and the wind whistling through the cabin like it was a harmonica, then the sound of Daddy crashing in through the door, and the smell of burning fish oil as he lit the lamp and stood over me in its yellow glow.

"Get dressed, Nathan," he said. "A schooner's run aground."

Beside me in bed, Grandpa grunted, rolled over, and pulled the blankets off me.

"I guess that means he's not coming," I said, sitting up.

"Let the old man sleep," Daddy said.

I was already dressed. The storm had chilled the cabin too much for me to get undressed the evening before. I pulled on the heavy slicker and rain hat Mr. Etheridge had given me when the surfmen got new ones in the autumn. I was surprised when we stepped outside to find the rain easing up and stars peeking out between the clouds.

Daddy suggested the privy. No sense pissing in the bushes when a gust of wind could blow the wrong way and make a mess of things. I ran ahead of Daddy, and the wet sand about froze my bare feet.

"They'll need help with the beach cart," I called over my shoulder.

Daddy's voice was swallowed in the wind, but he probably said that he'd catch up.

In the dark up ahead, I could see the Coston flare, the signal from the Pea Island surfmen to the stranded ship that help was on its way. Offshore, to the north, was the faint glow of a lantern—from the troubled ship, no doubt.

The men from the Pea Island station—all seven of them— were already pulling the beach cart toward the wreck. Its wooden wheels creaked as it rolled through the deep sand, and its contents—the Lyle gun, the faking box filled with rope, the shovels, pickax, sand anchor, and breeches buoy—all jostled and rattled in the big open wagon. I grabbed hold of a haul rope and added my muscles to theirs.

"Will you look at what the cat dragged in," said Mr. Bowser between panting breaths. Benjamin Bowser was the number-one surfman—first in rank after Mr. Etheridge, the keeper. He was tall and lanky, with hollowed-out cheeks and a bushy black mustache.

I grinned at Mr. Bowser. "Can I light the fuse for the Lyle gun?" I asked, knowing no one would let me.

"You hush and just pull," said Mr. Meekins sharply. Theodore Meekins was the widest of the crew, with hands like baseball mitts and serious, dark eyes. My face went hot when he reprimanded me. He was right. With a crew of men, and maybe even the captain's wife and children clinging to the grounded ship, I had no business jabbering like a fool. I tipped my head down and pulled with all my strength. Daddy joined us on the other side of the cart.

Over our heads, the clouds parted and stars glittered. To our right, the ocean thundered, inky black except for the white strips of the breakers and a dancing streak of light where the moon caught the waves. The stiff west wind whistled in my ears and turned my cheeks and hands icy cold.

When we reached the wreck, I could see the outline of a three-masted schooner. She was maybe two hundred yards from shore, lying on her side with her sails torn away. She tossed with each wave as if she was trying to free herself from the shoal but couldn't. On her slanting deck, I counted seven dark forms—the stranded sailors waiting for our help.

"Halt," Keeper Etheridge commanded. Then, in a loud, firm voice, "Action!"

The Pea Island crew moved like well-trained soldiers, and Daddy and I stood out of their way. Stanley Wise, William Irving, and Lewis Wescott grabbed the shovels and pick and began to dig a hole to bury the sand anchor. George Midgett and L. W. Tillett unloaded the faking box, pulled the shot line out of it, and wet a bight of the line in the ocean. Theodore Meekins unloaded the tall wooden crotch. It would be set up between the sand anchor and the wreck to hold the ropes above the surf. Richard Etheridge and Benjamin Bowser unloaded the Lyle gun, set it to aim at the ship, and got the flare ready to light the fuse on the gun.

The Lyle gun was ready to fire a weight and shot line over the wreck so the sailors could haul in the hawser line and fasten it to a mast. Then the breeches buoy—a pair of cutoff canvas breeches attached to a doughnut-shaped buoy—would be hauled out to the ship with a whip line and pulley, and one by one the sailors would be brought ashore, sitting in the breeches with the buoy holding them safely above the pounding sea.

Right when I expected to hear Richard Etheridge call "Ready" so we could hold our ears against the blast of the Lyle gun, instead I heard "Stop." We all stood still and looked out toward the wreck. The lantern was flashing—the long and short flashes of Morse code. I knew the code's letters, so I watched and read, ". . . i – t – e – w – a – i – t – u – n – t – i – l – d – a – y – l – i – t – e – w – a – i – t . . ." Wait. Wait until daylight.

I gazed out at the wounded ship. Mr. Meekins had told me that not one in a hundred sailors knows how to swim. They must be terrified, I thought, of the black, boiling sea at night.

Mr. Bowser let out a grunt of disapproval. "That schooner starts breaking up, they won't be hollering 'wait' anymore," he said.

Mr. Etheridge crossed his arms over his chest and frowned. The waves, taller than a man, rumbled in one at a time, each a powerful battering ram against the ship's hull. It was up to Mr. Etheridge to decide what was best to do. He stroked his white beard with work-worn fingers and squinted out at the ship. Finally, he sighed. "Get the surfboat," he ordered. "If the surf dies down, we'll use it instead of the breeches buoy."

Half the crew stayed with Keeper Etheridge to keep a watch on the ship, and Daddy and I followed the other three crew members back toward the station. As we walked, we heard shouts behind us. The seven crewmen from the Oregon Inlet station trotted to catch up.

"What did you do, lie abed for another two hours before you decided to come help?" Mr. Bowser chided.

"Your Pea Island crew has got to learn how to use the telephone right," said one of the Oregon Inlet crewmen. "I heard you wake up three other stations before you finally sounded our ring. We're *two* short and *one* long. . . ."

I wasn't sure which one of the Oregon Inlet crewmen was speaking. I'd only met them once before—their station was about five miles up the beach, and they were all white men and hard to tell apart in the dark. Just to make things more confusing, they had most of the same names as the Pea Island crew: Wescott and Midgett—they even had substitutes by the name of Meekins and Tillett, and their keeper was another Mr. Etheridge. Grandpa says they have the same surnames because back before the war the granddaddies and great-granddaddies of the Oregon Inlet crew used to *own* the granddaddies and great-granddaddies of the Pea Island crew, and they shared their family names with their slaves.

We got to the station, and two men pulled open the huge double doors so we could guide the surfboat, on its wheels, down the ramp to the beach. It was like a large rowboat, big enough for the whole crew of seven to row it and fit three or four sailors in to carry them back to shore. Mr. Meekins came out from the stables with one of the government team—the one who wasn't lame. Once she was hitched to the surfboat, we all took hold of the drag ropes and pulled like mules ourselves. Even with all those men, one mule, and one strong, but skinny, twelve-year-old boy pulling on the drag ropes, it still felt like we were trying to lug an entire steamer through a sea of molasses. By the time we rejoined the rest of the crew, sweat ran down my back and arms. My heart was pounding hard, too. Soon the rescue would begin.

The wind had shifted from west to northwest. The three-masted schooner looked like a cow struggling to birth a calf, lying on her side, rocking in the surf.

"She breaking up yet?" asked Mr. Bowser.

The sky had brightened, and I noticed a soft pink glow on the horizon. Daylight. Wait until daylight.

Richard Etheridge shouted, "Unload!" The Pea Island crew went into action with the surfboat, each man with his own job, unhitching the mule, pushing the surfboat to the edge of the sea, casting off the side lashings, taking off the wheels, lowering the boat onto the sand.

Within seconds, amid shouting of the commands "Take life preservers!" "Take oars!" and "Go!" the men had run the boat out into the breakers and jumped in. I held my breath as a huge wave crashed over the bow.

"Give way together!" Keeper Etheridge called. The oars moved in unison. Mr. Etheridge gripped the long steering oar. The surfboat faced the breakers head on and sliced through them. It moved swiftly over each towering wave toward the dark silhouette of the schooner.

The Oregon Inlet crew waited with Daddy and me. We watched as the surfboat reached the wreck.

In the eddy of calmer water on the lee side of the schooner, the surfmen were able to pull up close. A ladder had already been lowered, and the first of the sailors climbed down and reached out to be helped into the boat.

The sky turned light blue, and the pink glow spread until a speck of sun peeked up.

"Damn, if they're not loading their baggage as well!" Daddy said under his breath.

Four sailors had climbed safely into the surfboat, and a large crate was being lowered from the schooner's deck.

I frowned. Didn't they know these men were risking their lives to save them?

With the surfboat sitting low under its heavy load, the crew rowed back toward shore. The three remaining sailors watched, waiting for a second run.

Near shore, the surfboat got turned almost sideways. I yelped as a tall wave broke over its side and the men had to throw their weight to keep from capsizing. Daddy and I ran to the water and, with the Oregon Inlet crew, grabbed the sides of the boat and dragged it up onshore.

The sailors jumped out and scrambled up onto dry land as we unloaded the crate. Suddenly there was a tremendous crack, loud as a gunshot.

"She's breaking up!" someone yelled.

"Take oars!" Mr. Etheridge shouted. "Go!"

We shoved the surfboat back into the sea, and it crashed through the breakers, the men pulling hard at the oars. The sea would be rushing into the belly of the schooner now. Soon she would be in pieces. The captain and two sailors waved frantically. No one would be thinking of loading baggage now.

Another crack sounded, and the schooner lurched.

I watched the mast, willing it to stay intact until the men were safely out of its reach.

The sailors looked panicky. Two of them already clung to the ladder. As the surfboat approached them, one sailor tried to leap in too soon, missed, and had to be hauled in over the side, his legs flailing like a scared chicken. The other sailor, and finally the captain, always last, were loaded in, and the crew rowed furiously away from the wreck. Only when they were a safe distance away did I dare to take my eyes off the mast.

"You, boy, do you know where the teapot is at the station?" It took me a moment to realize one of the Oregon Inlet surfmen was talking to me.

"Yes, sir," I said.

"Let's go, then."

There was a creaking and a crash. When I turned to look at the wreck again, the mast had fallen.

I followed the surfman, and the four sailors followed us in tired silence.

At the station, I stoked the fire and pumped water for tea.

"I'm Mr. Forbes," said the surfman as he put six mugs and the steaming teapot on the table in front of the sailors. "And you are?"

We looked at them expectantly, and they looked at us.

All four of them had hair the color of sea oats—so blond it was almost white—and three of them had faces and hands as red as fish blood. I wondered if they were that color all over, or if it was just from the cold. They said nothing.

"Are you not from the States, then?" Mr. Forbes asked our guests.

They sipped their tea, folding their cold hands around the warm mugs. "Dank-ew," they each said, nodding.

Mr. Forbes sighed. I watched to see if the redness would go away as they warmed up.

So these were the Europeans Mr. Bowser had told me about—men from Poland, Sweden, Norway, and other countries from across the Atlantic who signed on as crewmen on American ships. They were white men but, Mr. Bowser said, had never been taught to treat a black man as less than a man. I smiled at them, and they smiled back.

There was the sound of approaching voices.

"I'd never have had you take the baggage if I'd known we were that close to breaking up," said a man with a Yankee accent.

"We can't thank you enough," said another Yankee. "The *Emma C. Cotton* will be a total loss, but you saved all men on board."

The schooner—the *Emma C. Cotton*—must have come from a port in a Northern state.

I helped Mr. Forbes and Pea Island's cook, Lewis Wescott, prepare a breakfast of bacon and biscuits for everyone. I carried the pot of hot coffee from the cookhouse to the main station house and stepped into the dining room. There, I stopped. The men were sitting around the table, helping themselves to the mounds of biscuits and thick slabs of bacon. All of the men: the Oregon Inlet crew, the Pea Island crew, Daddy, and the sailors. White men and black men sitting at table together. It was just like Mr. Bowser had told me it would be after a rescue on Pea Island.

"You going to bring that coffee over here or just stand there and wait for it to get cold?" Mr. Bowser called to me.

I hurried to the table with the pot, and Daddy handed me a plate full of food.

That wasn't the first time I felt it—the wanting to be a surfman—but I probably felt it then stronger than I ever had before. Stronger than when we lived on Roanoke Island and William, Floyd, and I did mock drills with an imaginary surfboat. Stronger than when Daddy, Grandpa, and I moved out here to Pea Island and I first watched the surfmen do their drills. Stronger than when Mr. Meekins said he'd teach me how to swim in the heavy surf.

On the way back to our cabin was the first time I said it to Daddy. Turns out I probably should have kept it to myself.

"Dammit, Nathan, you've got no appreciation for what I'm

giving you," he said. His round face had more lines in it than usual, and his shoulders, usually so square and strong, drooped a bit. "I've got us set up with our own boat and nets, working for ourselves. Would you rather work as a day laborer for pennies, the way most black folks have to?"

"No, I'd rather be a *surfman*," I said, knowing I should have bit my tongue and kept quiet, especially with Daddy so worn out.

We reached the cabin, and he yanked open the door and slammed it behind us.

"Nathan." He fixed me with his dark eyes. "There's a lot you don't understand . . . about the way things are. You won't ever be a surfman. Now put it out of your mind." He sniffed, smoothed his bristly mustache, and plopped onto his cot. I stared at him, my fists clenched. But this time I kept my mouth shut.

"Now let me get some sleep," he said, and turned his back to me.

Grandpa came in with an armload of brush for kindling and said he was going fishing since he was, apparently, the only one around here with sense enough to think about getting something for supper.

I lay on my bed and closed my eyes but didn't sleep. I was powerful angry at Daddy for telling me not to hope, and only wondering a little about those things he said I didn't understand.

TWO

So far, I've seen three dead people. The first was when I was six years old and Mamma's sister, Aunt Stella, tried to birth a baby. She and the baby both died, but she was the only one I saw, laid out in a pine box in the sitting room of her house. That was when we still lived in Elizabeth City, back on the North Carolina mainland.

The second dead person was the reason we left Elizabeth City. It was two years ago, when I was ten. One summer night, Daddy woke me, Mamma, and Grandpa well before dawn and said we were moving to Roanoke Island, where Mamma had cousins and where there was no Klan. We packed up quick, then shuffled through the dark streets toward Daddy's fishing skiff, carrying our belongings in crates and baskets. I kept asking why we were leaving. "Why, Daddy, why?" I kept after him, until he put down the crate he was carrying and took me by the hand. He told Mamma and Grandpa to wait and walked me past the Presbyterian church, out toward the Baker farm, to a quiet spot where a pin oak spread its branches against the night sky. Swinging from one of the branches, a rope around his neck, his ears and most of his fingers chopped off, was the Ames boy.

My legs went weak with the horror of it. I clutched Daddy's hand and cried.

"They don't need half a reason to lynch a man," Daddy said in a low growl. "Not even half."

I didn't ask one single more question about why we'd left our rented house without even telling the landlady, why we ran off in the night, or why we were moving to a place we'd only visited twice to see Mamma's cousins. All I needed to know was what Daddy had already said: we were going to where there was no Ku Klux Klan.

On Roanoke Island I went to school with the other colored children—the Berrys and Pughs and Bowsers. Miss Ella Midgett was already the teacher at the colored school, so Mamma couldn't get a job there, but Daddy said that was all right because he and Grandpa could just catch more fish.

That's where I first met the surfmen—the Pea Island crew, who each came to Roanoke Island one day a week on their day off to see their wives and children. Grandpa found out he and Daddy had already met the keeper of the Pea Island station,

Richard Etheridge, back when Mr. Etheridge was part of General Wild's African Brigade, which occupied Elizabeth City during the war.

That's also where I got to know William and Floyd, two boys from school. William was older than me, about fourteen or so, and Floyd a little younger than me. They taught me how to swim in the Croatan Sound, off the west side of the island near where we lived. They were both related to surfmen—nephews or cousins or something—and told me how they both wanted to become surfmen when they turned eighteen. They'd puff up their chests and recite the surfman's motto: "You have to go out, but you don't have to come back."

William's family had a rickety old rowboat, and when it wasn't being used for fishing or oystering or taking William's uncle back and forth to his job at the fish market in Wanchese, William and Floyd and I snuck away with it. We rowed it to the northern part of the island, landed where there were hardly any houses, and pretended we were surfmen. "Take life preservers!" William would shout. "Take oars! Go!" We'd shove the rowboat back into the water, leap in, and row furiously out to an imagined wreck, William and Floyd each with an oar and me with a long stick. We welcomed phantom stranded sailors, who were always nearly dead and very glad to see us, loaded them into our "surfboat," and took them back to shore. Sometimes we practiced capsize drills—took the rowboat out into the deep water and tipped it over on purpose, the way the surfmen sometimes did on Tuesdays during their regular boat drills. We'd swim around and struggle with the boat until we got it righted again and the oars collected.

All that fun with the boat ended the day Floyd got hit in the head as the boat capsized. He was knocked out cold, and William and I had to hold him up so he wouldn't drown, and keep hold of the boat so it wouldn't drift away. Floyd took the longest time to come to, and by then the current had pulled us almost down to where all the houses were. We tried to right the boat and get out of there before anyone saw, but Mr. Ward spotted us with the boat still capsized and told our parents. We'd also lost an oar, which washed up two days later, and Floyd looked like he'd been bitten in the head by a shark, so there wasn't much use trying to keep it all a secret. After that, when we wanted to do surfboat rescues, we stayed on dry land and only pretended we had a boat, because not one of the three of us wanted to get another whipping like we each got that night.

The third dead person I saw was Mamma. One day last spring, she took to her bed with her throat so swelled up and sore she could hardly talk and her eyes bulging out like poached eggs. Daddy called on Doc Fearing, but he said it was the diphtheria and she was too far gone for him to help her. Two days later, she was dead.

Losing Mamma was the most sorrowful thing that has ever

happened to me. For weeks I'd wake up thinking I felt her cool hand against my cheek, and when I'd open my eyes and realize it couldn't be true, my chest about caved in with the sadness of it.

After we buried Mamma, Daddy didn't want to stay on Roanoke Island anymore. He didn't want to go back to Elizabeth City either, so when Mr. Etheridge said there was a fisherman's cabin on Pea Island near the station that hadn't been used for a long time, Daddy figured that was as good an invitation as we needed to move out here.

The cabin needed a lot of repair when we first came, but it had a stove, two beds, a table, and a few chairs. There was already a rain barrel under the eaves that was nice and full from early summer rains, and after a little fixing up, the privy was just fine. We built the smokehouse from salvaged wood and started burying fish heads in the sand to prepare a garden plot. Next spring we'll put up our garden fence, to keep the cows and wild ponies out, and our homestead will be complete.

Still, the cabin always feels like it's missing Mamma. I keep thinking I'll see her picking her way through the thick brush toward our front door, asking why did we up and move to the edge of the earth just because we couldn't find her for a while. And I wonder where she went—what it feels like to live in "God's house," like the preacher in Elizabeth City used to talk about.

I know Daddy's missing Mamma, too, even though he doesn't say it. It seems like he put a hard mask on his face—a mask that doesn't show whether he's sad or scared anymore but makes him look strong all the time, with his jaw set and his eyes steady like they're staring right through you to tomorrow. Grandpa says some folks grieve that way and Daddy will come around, just give him time. It hasn't even been a year yet since we lost Mamma.

When we first got here, especially on days when Daddy seemed like he couldn't stand to be around another living soul, I went off by myself to explore the island—all eight miles long and one mile across of it. I walked along the beach down to New Inlet on the southern end of the island and could just barely see the red roof of the New Inlet Life-Saving Station on the other side of the channel. I burrowed into the quiet stands of weather-beaten pine, cedar, and oak trees and tracked raccoons and foxes in the sand. I went all the way to the north end of the island, where the bright red Oregon Inlet station sits near a cluster of hunting cabins, empty in the summer. If I was there at dusk, I could see the Bodie Island lighthouse flashing on the other side of Oregon Inlet. Then, of course, there's the Pea Island station, about two miles up from the southern end of the island and just north of our cabin. Its siding is painted cornflower blue but its roof and trim are vermilion, which makes it so sailors can see it from far out in the ocean.

I also found swampy places on the sound side and white sand beach on the ocean side, and a herd or two of cows and wild ponies in between. The ponies are descendants of the ponies that swam ashore from wrecked Spanish ships years and years ago. With no one to take care of them, they all have patchy hair from chewing on flea bites and potbellies from worms.

The only other thing I found, besides the telegraph poles that run the length of the island, was the ruins of the old Etheridge house. Mr. Bowser said Mr. Jesse Etheridge, one of the white Etheridges, used to live in it, but that nobody has tried to fix it up since a northeaster blew most of the roof off some years ago.

When the surfmen came back to the station on August first after their summer break, I took to watching their drills from a sand hill nearby. They did them in the morning: drilling with the surfboat on Tuesday, practicing with the signal flags on Wednesday, breeches-buoy drill on Thursday, and resuscitation of the apparently drowned on Friday. Saturday was general cleaning, Sunday a day of rest except for keeping watch, and some days they had a fire drill. Mondays were used for different things, like having the mules practice pulling the surfboat, overhauling the beach apparatus equipment, or whitewashing the stables. Then, in the afternoons, the man on watch for the day stayed on the lookout deck atop the station, and the rest of the crew went hunting or fishing.

One Friday, I was watching from my usual spot when they started motioning me to come on down from my sand hill. I about froze up, scared that they were mad at me for watching so often. But then Mr. Etheridge called out, "William says he's tired of being victim"—he pointed at Mr. Irving, the lowest-ranking surfman—"and the men need practice with a child victim, anyway. Come on down here."

Mr. Etheridge is the kind of man who, if he tells you to do something, you do it. I walked slowly toward the surfmen.

"All you've got to do is start out apparently drowned and end up alive," said Mr. Wise, grinning. "We'll do the rest."

"And your ribs'll feel fine after a few days," said Mr. Irving.

I raised my eyebrows. My ribs? But I didn't have time to start worrying, because all of a sudden the men went into action, and instead of working on the surfboat or the breeches buoy, they started working on *me*.

They pushed me down in the sand on my back. "He's not breathing," someone cried. "Begin resuscitation! Wipe dry the mouth and nostrils!"

I was about to yell that I was breathing just fine, but somebody stuck a dry rag in my mouth and then wiped my nose with it, and I was too surprised to yell anything. They about tore the buttons off my shirt to open it up and slapped me on the chest three times *hard*.

"Ow!" I cried.

"There's no response, proceed to step two!" someone shouted.

Since when is "Ow" not a response? I wondered. They pried my mouth open and stuck a piece of cork between my teeth.

"What's this for?" I tried to ask, but it came out sounding like "Huh-ih-haw?" and nobody answered me.

They rolled me onto my stomach over top of a bundled-up blanket, and somebody shoved against my back so hard the blanket about squashed my stomach up flat against my backbone.

"He's got a lot of seawater running out his mouth. Keep pushing!" they shouted.

I could have told them that was drool, but I didn't want to try talking again with the cork between my teeth.

After pushing on my back a few more times, somebody said the seawater was done running out, and they rolled me onto my back again. Three of them knelt around me—Mr. Pugh, Mr. Wise, and Mr. Bowser. "We've got to move to step three," said Mr. Wise, looking worried, "or we'll lose him for sure."

I winced. Step three was probably even worse than steps one and two.

Mr. Pugh took out the cork, then used a handkerchief to grab my tongue and hold it out the corner of my mouth. Mr. Bowser held my arms up over my head, and Mr. Wise commenced to push me below the ribs like he was trying to squeeze the entire contents of my chest out through the top of my head.

"One, two, three," they all counted while Mr. Wise pushed. Then, "One, two, three," they said as he waited between pushes.

They counted and pushed and counted and pushed until Mr. Bowser said, "I think he's starting to breathe!"

I could have breathed a whole lot better if they'd have taken that handkerchief off my tongue and stopped mashing my chest, but I guess being the victim means you have to try and breathe *despite* being resuscitated.

Mr. Wise stopped pushing. "He's breathing on his own!" he announced.

Mr. Bowser let go my arms, Mr. Pugh let go my tongue, and everybody cheered.

"You see? We saved you," said Mr. Irving.

I sat up and touched my sore ribs. "That being resuscitated seems mostly as bad as drowning," I said.

They all laughed.

After that day, the surfmen treated me like I was one of their own nephews—teasing me about being so skinny, calling me over to help tote water to the stables, sending me to tell Daddy and Grandpa they should come to the station house to play cards after supper. And it only took three days for my ribs to stop hurting.

September seemed to bring in even more mosquitoes, stinging yellow flies, and sand fleas. But in October I stopped itching quite so much, and the figs on the bush in front of the station got ripe and were about the best thing I'd ever tasted.

Some days I helped Daddy in the fishing skiff, and some days Grandpa and I took handlines and fished in the ocean, standing at the edge with waves washing over our legs. Some days I helped the surfmen, especially when the supply boat came in with their meat, canned goods, and other supplies and it all had to be unloaded. And some days I took one of Daddy's old copies of the *Fisherman and Farmer* newspaper and sat with my back propped up against the outside of the smokehouse to read. On those days I usually missed Roanoke Island and school and tried to guess what William and Floyd were doing. I wondered if Mamma would be disappointed that I wasn't in school anymore. She used to say it was "a god-awful shame" how many children, both black and white, left school and started working at age ten and hardly even learned to read. Mamma taught me how to read even before I started school, and Miss Ella Midgett, my teacher on Roanoke Island, said I was the best reader in the whole class. At least I went to school until I turned eleven.

One afternoon in early November, I went to the station to see if there was anything interesting going on. The sky was blue as Mamma's china, and a strong northeast wind blew spray off the tops of the waves and made them glitter in the sunshine. The waves went every which way because of the wind and rumbled loud as a railroad train as they crashed onshore.

At first I thought it was a pelican bobbing in the rough surf. Then I let out a yelp, because I saw that it was a man's head.

I ran, shouting, to the station. "Mr. Etheridge! Mr. Bowser! Come quickly, someone is drowning!" I yelled.

Mr. Bowser came out of the stables, a curry brush in his hand.

"You're talking nonsense, boy," he said. "Don't you think the man on watch would see a drowning from up on the lookout deck well before you could see it standing down here on those short little stubby legs of yours?"

"But I *saw* it!" I insisted. "There's someone in the surf!" I didn't care how ridiculous he thought I was being. I grabbed his arm and dragged him toward the ocean.

Mr. Bowser squinted in the bright sunlight out at the waves and started to laugh. "I tell you one thing, boy, and don't you forget it. You ever see *that* nappy head floating in the ocean, you *know* he's not drowned. That's Theodore Meekins, and he can outswim any man—or fish, I reckon. He's probably out there racing the dolphins right now."

He turned to go back to the stables, and I stared with my mouth open as Mr. Meekins dove under a towering wave. The wave broke and sent spray flying into the sky. On the other side of the trough, there was Mr. Meekins, raising his arms to dive under again.

As I watched, I felt the power of it—the sea trying to drown Mr. Meekins and him fighting it. We hadn't been able to fight the Klan—they'd won and scared us into leaving our home. And we hadn't been able to fight the disease Mamma got. It won and took Mamma away from us. But people called the surfmen "heroes of the surf" and "storm warriors," because they fought the sea, wind, and storms, and brought sailors back safely. Over and over again, they won the battle. I wanted to fight battles like that—and win.

When Mr. Meekins came up onshore, with beads of water gleaming on his broad chest and his cutoff breeches dripping onto the sand, I asked if he would teach me to swim in the waves like that. He looked me up and down, like maybe I was still too skinny and puny to win in a battle against the ocean. "Why don't you eat plenty of red drum for Thanksgiving and lots of fig pudding at Christmas," he said. "And when the water starts to warm up again in spring, we'll see what we can do."

I grinned real big.

At both Thanksgiving and Christmas, which we spent with Mamma's cousins on Roanoke Island, everyone commented on what a good appetite I had.

Then, on December 27, when the *Emma C. Cotton* ran aground and I helped with the rescue of the seven-man crew, I felt like I'd fought in a battle and won.

THREE

A couple of days after the *Emma C. Cotton* wrecked, we'd run out of cornmeal and coal, so it was time for us to go to the town of Manteo on Roanoke Island for supplies.

I lowered the bucket into our rain barrel and hit ice. I would have asked Daddy and Grandpa to help me move it inside, but they were busy arguing, and I figured the sun would melt it by the time we got back from Roanoke Island anyway. The two carp we'd put in it to keep it clean and eat the wigglers in summer didn't seem to mind. They just swam around under the ice like it was any other day.

"Come on now. Just one extra dollar is all I'm asking for," I heard Grandpa insisting.

"That's what I'm telling you. None of them are *extra*," Daddy shot back.

"You giving up on your poor mother so fast? How's she going to find us here if we don't let her know?"

"Fast? So *fast?*" Daddy's voice rose in frustration. "It's been thirty-five years!" Then, more gently, he said, "Don't you think it's time to let it rest, Papa?"

There was silence from inside. Then, "No. I'm not ready to give up. And all I want is one dollar."

Daddy didn't say anything, but I knew he was handing Grandpa a dollar bill and giving him a look like he wished he hadn't.

I burst into the cabin. "I can't wash because the water's frozen, so I'm ready to go."

The sun had just peeked up into a cloudless sky. The brisk southwest wind would make it easy for us to sail to Roanoke Island and back in one day, as long as it stayed fresh. We'd spent the two days before hunting, and had hung about thirty ruddy ducks and Canada geese on the outside of the cabin to cool overnight. These Daddy would trade at Griffin, Sample & Company General Store for the things we needed: coal and wood, cornmeal and sweet potatoes, shot and powder for the shotgun, and new line for repairing the fishing nets.

Daddy inspected my face and hands. "Frozen water, huh?"

I nodded.

He took the rag off the nail in the kitchen and stuffed it in his pocket. I hadn't escaped washing so easily. "Let's go, then," he said.

We carried the birds to the sound side of the island, where the skiff was moored, and loaded them into the boat. Daddy dipped a corner of the rag into the frigid sound water and handed it to me. It made my face, neck, and hands feel like ice—salty ice. Daddy and Grandpa splashed water on their own faces, and I shivered watching them.

We hoisted our sails, and the wind filled them. The boat skimmed across the Pamlico Sound, slapping the chop and making me feel like I was flying. When Daddy called, "Coming about," we tacked to the north, and the low green bumps of the trees on Roanoke Island came into view.

As we sailed closer, I remembered how Roanoke Island used to seem so small. Compared to Elizabeth City, Manteo had seemed lonely, with its few weather-beaten houses and stunted trees. But now, after the isolation of Pea Island, Manteo felt like a bustling town.

We sailed into Shallowbag Bay and docked in Manteo, then walked down the sandy street toward Griffin, Sample & Company. We skirted Mr. Ward's oxcart and waved to him as best we could while carrying all those dead birds. We saw a few other folks we'd gotten to know in the time we'd lived there and said hello. Mrs. Leary, the teacher from the white school, stopped and asked us how we were faring. We politely said, "Fine."

Once the birds were delivered, Grandpa and I left Daddy to

haggle over price with Mr. Griffin, and we went to the post office. Grandpa slapped three pennies down on the counter.

"Mr. Brothers, I need a sheet of writing paper, an envelope, and postage," he told the postman.

"Morning, Ulysses," Mr. Brothers said, smiling. "And I suppose Nathan will want to borrow my pen and ink as well?"

We both nodded.

Two white women came in, and Grandpa and I waited while Mr. Brothers took care of them first. When finally the office was empty, Mr. Brothers brought me the paper, envelope, pen, and ink. Grandpa dictated as I wrote:

"Please put this advertisement in your newspaper: 'My dearest Dahlia. We have moved to Pea Island on the Outer Banks of North Carolina. To find us, inquire at the Pea Island Life-Saving Station. We anxiously await your return. Your loving husband, son, and grandson, Ulysses, George, and Nathan Williams.' "

I addressed the envelope to the *Missionary Record* in Raleigh, North Carolina, and stuck the letter and Grandpa's dollar inside. We said good day to Mr. Brothers and went outside into the cold sunshine.

"Did I ever tell you about my Saturday nights with your Grandma Dahlia?" Grandpa asked.

"No, I don't believe you have," I said. We both knew that was a lie—I'd heard the story lots of times—but I did want to hear it again.

Grandpa's eyes lit up, the way they always did when he told that story. We leaned against a hitching post, and Grandpa tipped his head back, remembering. "Lord, she was a beauty, your grandma. Long, graceful legs like a doe, and lips soft like roses. She smelled like roses, too, on account of her mistress—Mistress Callie they called her—said her husband had given her more rose water than she could use up before she died, so she gave a bottle of it to my Dahlia. Saturday nights she'd come walking from Mistress Callie's farm—wasn't but about two miles away—and I could smell those roses even before I could see her. I'd quick pump some water and wash up, trying to smell a little better myself, you know, after working in the fields all day." He laughed and shook his head. "I'd shout to my kinfolk to get on out of our cabin, saying 'Me and my Dahlia, we gonna have us a time!'" He lifted his face to the sun and let it shine on his closed eyes. The lines on his cheeks and forehead smoothed out as he drifted in his memory back to the past. "And Lord, we did have us a time, too," he said softly. Then, suddenly, he seemed to startle into the present. He rubbed the gray stubble of his beard. "What's all this your daddy's trying to tell me, about how folks up and started new families when they got sold away, and forgot about their old families? Your grandma would never do that! I've never even looked at another woman since she's been gone— well, hardly. And I know she's coming back. I *know* it. I can feel it in my bones."

I raised my eyebrows at him. "Does it feel like the rheumatism, Grandpa?" I asked.

He slapped me upside the head, gently.

"She'll come, Grandpa," I said, touching his hand. "One of these days she'll see your advertisement in the newspaper, and she'll show up at our cabin."

He nodded.

"And will you shoo me and Daddy out of the cabin and say, 'Me and my Dahlia, we gonna have us a time!'?"

He tapped my knee, grinning. "That's just *exactly* what I'll say."

Just then I heard voices and giggling.

"Nathan!"

I turned my head.

"See, it *is* him. I told you so."

It was William and Floyd with their sisters. Floyd's sister, Fannie, was about my age, and William's sister, Seabright, was only seven, with lively braids that stuck out every which way.

Grandpa said he'd leave me to visit with my friends and he'd go find Daddy.

"Nathan, did you see the *Emma C. Cotton* break up?" Fannie ran to me and stood, breathless, waiting for an answer. Her black braids framed her high forehead and wide-set eyes.

"Did you help with the rescue?" Seabright asked. "Did you row out in the surfboat?"

William and Floyd stood over to the side. William had grown taller since I'd last seen him. He was lanky, with arms and legs like mooring poles. Floyd had grown stockier. They both looked as if they were brooding.

"I helped pull the beach cart and the surfboat, but I didn't row out," I said.

"Was everyone almost killed?" Fannie wanted to know.

"Was it scary?" Seabright asked. She twisted the edge of her dress around her slender fingers.

I remembered the huge wave breaking over the bow of the surfboat as it made its way out, and then the sound of the mast crashing into the water just moments after the crew was safely away.

"Yes," I said. "But it was probably scariest for the sailors, since none of them knew how to swim." I looked at William and Floyd. "Mr. Meekins is going to teach me how to swim in the heavy surf."

William scuffed his toes in the sand and Floyd just grunted.

"They're sore because you got to help with the rescue and they didn't," Fannie said.

"I am not," Floyd snapped. "It doesn't matter anyway, because Nathan's just a helper—a fisherman volunteer. William and me, we'll be *real* surfmen, right, William?"

William pulled up a weed and chewed on the end. "Of course that's right," he said coolly.

I knew better than to argue with two boys who were bigger than me. I'd had enough of arguing with Daddy about this very same thing, anyway.

"We're coming to the auction," said Fannie, obviously changing the subject.

"Me too," said Seabright.

The auction of the wrecked *Emma C. Cotton*—broken-up timbers, sails, and any of her load of coal they'd been able to salvage—was scheduled for the second of January or the first good sailing day after that.

"I'll see you there, then," I said.

Daddy and Grandpa walked toward us carrying our sacks of groceries. Floyd, William, and I took the sacks out of their arms and loaded them into our skiff.

Daddy asked the children about their families. Fannie said her and Floyd's mother had been out crabbing a couple of days ago, cut her foot on a shell, and now she was in bed with her foot swelled up.

"Has she put turpentine and fat meat on it?" Daddy asked.

"Yes, sir," said Fannie.

"Has your Papa called on Doc Fearing?" he asked.

Fannie looked down at her toes in the sand. "You know how it is around here with black folks and Doc Fearing. Nobody goes until it's too late, so they think if you call on him, you're liable to die before sunup." She looked up at Daddy, her eyes pained. "I wish we had our own colored doctor the way you had in Elizabeth City."

Daddy started to untie our mooring rope. "You tell your papa to call on Doc Fearing sooner rather than later, you hear?"

Fannie and Floyd both nodded.

"I'll come see your mamma next time I'm on the island," he said. "Tell her I hope she feels better."

Grandpa and I sent our regards, too.

The afternoon light was slanting low. We all said our goodbyes and hoisted our sails. The southwest wind was even stronger than before, and we skimmed easily across the water.

I wanted to ask Grandpa why Floyd and William were so sure they'd be surfmen and I wouldn't. But I dared not bring up that particular subject in front of Daddy.

"That Mr. Griffin robbed us again—fifty cents a pair for those birds!" Daddy scowled, and his bushy eyebrows nearly met in the middle. "He's got some nerve, when I *know* he pays a dollar a pair to any white man who walks into that store."

Grandpa shook his head. "And there's not a blessed thing you can do about it, so you better get sixty birds next time instead of thirty and stop your complaining."

Daddy shot him an angry glare, and they both fell silent.

The sun glowed red behind low clouds as it sank toward sunset. We sped along, the wind pushing us with a steady hand. We'd be home before dark.

fOUR

"It's just always been a family thing," Grandpa explained. He was picking the berries out of a pile of yaupon leaves, getting ready to make yaupon tea. His gray hair stuck out in thick tufts, and his voice was raspy with early-morning rustiness. "The Bowsers, Tilletts, Midgetts, Berrys, Etheridges—the white families and the black families—they've been in the Life-Saving Service for a while now, and it just stays in the family, I suppose." A beetle scurried across the table. Grandpa knocked it onto the floor and squashed it with his foot.

"Couldn't they ever let a new person in?" I asked.

Grandpa just shrugged. "Go dump these berries outside," he said, and handed me a pot half full of berries. I scrunched up my nose—the only thing yaupon berries are good for is to make you throw up.

When I came back in, Grandpa told me to set the pot down and sit myself down. Then he leaned forward. "What's wrong with fishing?" he asked, his face serious.

"Nothing's *wrong* with it. I guess I just . . ." I ran my thumbnail down a groove in the table. "I guess I want to hope for something better, that's all."

Grandpa patted my hand and nodded. "Then you keep on hoping, boy. Why, it's my hopes of finding your grandma that have kept me going all these years." He scooped up the pile of yaupon leaves.

My chest went hollow with dread. I saw myself with white hair and an old, raspy voice saying, "Someday I want to be a surfman."

"No, Grandpa!" I brought my fist down hard. "I don't want to just hope. I want to *do* it!"

Grandpa stared at me, startled.

I ran out of the cabin into the gray, windless day. I breathed in the cold air and tried to calm down. What would Mamma say if she were here? "Nathan, you can do anything you set your mind to." That's what she'd say. I closed my eyes and tried to hear her voice. I could see her in my mind's eye, an apron covering the front of her faded green dress, wagging one flour-dusted finger at me. "Don't expect it to be easy, Nathan, because it *won't*."

"Okay, Mamma," I whispered. "I won't."

• • •

The crew of the *Emma C. Cotton* stayed at the station for three days. Then Mr. Etheridge hitched the government team to the driving cart and drove them up to Oregon Inlet so they could take a steamer to Norfolk. The captain, Mr. Ayres, stayed behind, and when the surf finally went calm again, the surfmen helped him gather the topsails, stores, and whatever else they could salvage off the ship.

On the day of the auction, buyers came from Manteo, Hatteras, Ocracoke, and Nags Head. The day was foggy and rainy, and everyone stood out under umbrellas while the Commissioner of Wrecks, one of the white Mr. Meekinses, called out prices and announced things "sold." The salvaged timbers, sails, line, and what was left of the stores of coal were auctioned off to the highest bidder. Mr. Ayres said that before the wreck it had all been worth over ten thousand dollars. He hoped to get at least a hundred dollars out of the auction to bring back to the boat's owner.

Mr. Bowser told me that on a sunny day an auction easily turned into a picnic, but the rain didn't make good picnic weather. Fannie had stayed home to help her mother, whose foot was healing slowly, and Seabright hadn't been allowed to come in the rain, but William and Floyd were there. They sidled up to me, each of them holding a coat over his head.

"Nathan, can you get us in to see the beach cart and surfboat?" William whispered.

I frowned. "We're not supposed to go snooping around the boat room," I said. "That equipment is for drills and rescues only."

"Come on." William gave me a little shove. "Everyone is busy here. No one will know. We just want to look."

"Yeah," said Floyd. "We'll be back before anyone sees we're gone."

I shook my head, ready to object again. William looked at me scornfully. "I thought you did everything around here—help with rescues, eat with the surfmen, learn to swim in the heavy surf—and you're telling me you're not even allowed to *look* at the equipment while it's sitting in the station?"

I straightened my shoulders. "Oh, fine," I said impatiently. "We can go, but just for a minute."

We ran down the beach, through the cold, wet sand, to the station house. We were plenty far enough away from the auction that no one would see us. And because of the fog, the surfmen were walking patrols today rather than keeping watch from the lookout deck. The station house was deserted.

We walked up the boat ramp, and I unlatched the huge double doors and pulled on one. It slid aside with a loud creak. The three of us stepped inside the dimly lit boat room.

William ran his hand over the side of the surfboat. Floyd went to the beach cart and touched the sleek Lyle gun. I kept watch at the door.

"In a few years, this is where I'll be," said William. "Doing drills, working the rescues—"

"That's if someone retires," Floyd interrupted him.

"Half of them are old codgers," William shot back. "Somebody will retire."

"A few years after William joins the crew, I'll be old enough as well," I announced.

They both looked at me. William scoffed. "Old enough for what? To pull in the nets for your daddy?"

I took a step toward him. "I *live* here." I jabbed my finger into his ribs for emphasis. "I've already done a rescue. You've only *played* at rescues."

William shoved me hard. "You're *nobody*. When me and Floyd are surfmen, *if* we let you, you can *help*."

I shoved him back. "I'll be a surfman first. I'll be a higher rank than you."

William grasped the front of my shirt and got up in my face. "Not on my grandfather's grave," he hissed.

I jerked free, but wasn't prepared for what happened next. William took one step back, cocked his elbow, and slammed his fist into my face. Pain shot through my cheekbone and left eye. I staggered for just an instant, then swung and sent my own balled fist into William's jaw. He spat and I saw the blood dribble down his chin. Then he came at me again but collided with Floyd.

"Are you *crazy?*" Floyd stood between us, his eyes wild and scared. "Dorman Pugh is up the beach—he's coming back from patrol."

We scrambled for the doorway. William and Floyd took off running. I slid the heavy door back into place, then jumped off the boat ramp and ran back to the auction, rain drenching my face and cooling my temper. William and Floyd had already rejoined their families, as if nothing had happened.

Before long, my cheekbone started to feel like it was stuffed with cotton. I decided to leave before anyone noticed the swelling.

Back at our cabin, I soaked a rag in cold water and held it to my face. Tomorrow I would have a shiner. What would I tell Daddy?

The door opened, and Grandpa walked in. "William's lip is still bleeding. I came to see how bad you look," he said.

I held the rag away from my cheek, and Grandpa bent to get a good look. He whistled. "That'll be one of the best shiners North Carolina has ever seen, I reckon."

I laughed a little, which made my face hurt more.

"You want to tell me what happened?" he asked.

I sighed. "No."

He pulled up a chair and sat down. "Well, tell me anyway," he said. He folded his bony fingers together and set his hands on the table, like he had all day to wait for me to talk and wasn't going to move until I did.

I told him about how much I wanted to be a surfman, how helping to save those sailors felt like I'd done something big, something great, like I'd fought a battle and won, and how there are no battles to fight as a fisherman, just the same nets day after day. I told him how I thought Mamma would encourage me to dream big, to work hard for what I wanted, but how everyone was mad at me for wanting it—Floyd, William, even Daddy.

Grandpa listened without interrupting. When I was done, he said, "I'd shoot myself before I'd tell you not to hope. And if you work real hard, you ought to get what it is you're wanting. But you've got to be ready in case what you hope for doesn't come looking the way you think it should." He lifted up his hat, scratched his head, and put his hat back on. "Did I ever tell you how I used to have a hankering for a piece of land?"

I shook my head no.

Grandpa nodded.

"It wasn't during slavery times, of course, but after the war, when I had my freedom. Master Johnson had given me some coins when I left his place, and what I wanted more than anything was a farm—just a small one, with a little cottage on it— so I could work the land like I'd always done, knew how to do, only do it for myself instead of for Master Johnson." He shook his head slightly. "But then one thing led to another, the way life does, and at some point I knew I was never going to have that farm, never going to live in a house that belonged to me." He looked up at me. "And you know what?" he asked.

"What?" I echoed.

"It has all been just fine. I certainly enjoyed hoping for that piece of land. And by the time I knew I was never going to get it, I had other good things instead." He knitted his eyebrows together, like he was trying to figure out the best way to explain things. "What I wanted from that farm was independence—I didn't want to work for another man, white or black, ever again. And I wanted to work it with someone I loved: your Grandma Dahlia. What I got was a fishing skiff. Around here, having your own boat is just like having land—you don't have to work for anybody but yourself. And I got to work that skiff with someone I love—your daddy, and then after a while, you. So, you see, sometimes your dreams show up dressed a little different than you thought they'd be. You have to know how to recognize them when they get there."

I nodded.

Grandpa got a faraway look in his eyes. "When your grandma comes back, we'll just have to teach her how to fish now, won't we?"

I laughed, and Grandpa gave me a mischievous grin. "And someday I *will* have a piece of land. Just a very small one." He said it like he was giving away a secret.

"How will you do that, Grandpa?" I asked.

"When they bury me, that piece of land will be *mine*. I'll have a piece six feet by two feet that nobody else can claim but me."

"Grandpa!" I frowned at him and jostled his arm. "Don't talk like that!"

"I'm just looking at the bright side," he insisted.

I was still giving him a perturbed look.

"Stop your worrying," he said. He took the rag out of my hand, dipped it into the basin of cool water, then pressed it against my cheek again. "You'll be grown and probably have young ones of your own before I'll let anyone even think about burying me."

"Good," I said.

"But I don't see any harm in you hoping to be a surfman," he said. "And working hard toward it and all."

That night I heard Grandpa and Daddy outside the cabin arguing. The ocean was loud and almost drowned out their voices, but I could still tell the argument was about me because I heard them say "the boy" several times. And from the sounds of it, Daddy *did* see harm in me hoping to become a surfman.

fIVE

Even after the auction, coal from the *Emma C. Cotton* washed up onshore, a little at a time. One morning, Daddy took up a sack and told me we were going to gather coal so we'd have less to buy in Manteo next time. I knew he was also wanting to talk, to ease the silent anger that had stood guard between us since the night he'd argued with Grandpa about me.

He gave me the sack to carry, and he, for some reason, carried a fifteen-pound red drum he'd hooked by the gills and tied a line to. I looked at the fish, swinging on the line as Daddy walked, its dead eyes staring blankly. But I didn't ask Daddy why he was taking it along.

We made our way through the brush to the shore, then turned north. The day was cloudy, the wind light, and the ocean calm and dull green. As we started up the beach, the seagulls screamed overhead and circled Daddy and his fish. The sand-pipers ran in and out of the waves onshore, pecking at the sand for food.

I gathered the lumps of coal where they lay scattered by the receding tide and dumped them into the sack. We walked in silence, the dead fish swinging, and Daddy looking like he was figuring something in his head, frowning a little, and squinting into the glare of the white sky. I was leaning over to pick up a piece of coal when Daddy grabbed my shoulder and said, "Watch."

He dropped the red drum on the sand near the water's edge, then moved back from it and motioned for me to sit with him.

Screaming seagulls flocked to the drum and attacked it. They ripped through the skin and pecked the flesh with their strong beaks until fish guts and blood stained the sand. The hungry birds pecked at each other, too. The stronger ones squawked and flew at the weaker ones, scaring them away from the precious food. One of the gulls—one that never made it close enough to the fish to get a bite—had only one leg. I wondered if he'd lost it in a fight over food this way.

"They don't know how to share," I said.

"They can't share," said Daddy. "There's only one fish." He flattened out the sand between us with his palm. "There's not enough to go around."

I watched the birds again and saw that he was right. There was not much left of the drum now except bones, guts, and head.

And what seemed like hundreds of gulls still flapped and squawked at each other, trying to grab the last bits of flesh.

"It's what I've been trying to tell you," said Daddy. "About you wanting to be a surfman."

I snapped my head around to face him.

"I better explain it to you before you get yourself beat up again . . . like those birds over there." He jerked his chin toward the one-legged gull.

"It used to be that a black man could apply for a job in the Life-Saving Service in North Carolina, and if he was qualified, he could be assigned to most any station."

I nodded. I knew Mr. Etheridge had come to Pea Island from the Oregon Inlet station and Mr. Wescott had come from Caffeys Inlet Station.

"They usually kept the black men in the lowest-ranking positions—number six or seven on the roster—but the whites and blacks worked together. Those were the 'checkerboard' crews," he said. "That was in the 1870s, when the Life-Saving Service first started."

The birds were beginning to disperse now, finding nothing more to eat.

"That was back when we thought the war had changed everything and we'd finally get the respect we deserved." Daddy stared out at the dull green ocean.

"But now they've made Mr. Etheridge keeper," I said. "That's the highest position. And Mr. Bowser is the number-one surf-man, and Mr. Midgett is number two. . . ." My voice trailed off when I saw the anger in Daddy's face.

"And there are no black surfmen at any other North Carolina stations," he snapped. The blood throbbed in his temple, and his jaw clenched tight. "The whites don't want to work with colored men anymore, so they've put all the blacks here, and there's no place else to go." He picked up a scallop shell and flung it at a squawking gull. "They've got eighteen stations for the whites. Some of those surfmen can't even read or write, and some hardly know the drills or how to swim. And you've got every black boy on Roanoke Island growing up wanting to be a surf-man, learning to swim, training himself in the drills, and knowing that one of the Pea Island crew will have to get sick or die before he can get the job."

I looked at the drum carcass lying in the sand. "It's like they've thrown us one fish," I said quietly. "So we can fight over it."

Daddy nodded.

The last gulls circled overhead, then flew off.

"You leave the dreams of being a surfman to the boys from Roanoke Island. Most of them won't even get what they want. It's only the sons and nephews of the surfmen who will get the few jobs." Daddy rose, picked up the drum carcass, and threw it out as far as he could into the water. "Fishermen have always helped with the rescues, so you can keep on with that." He looked at me and frowned. "And someday you'll get it through your fool head that having your own boat and nets is a damn good way to earn a living."

"I *know* it's a good way, Daddy. . . ." I hadn't meant to be ungrateful.

I had wanted to hope for more than being a fisherman. But if Daddy was right, that wanting to be a surfman just wasn't my dream to have, then I might as well give it up the way Grandpa had given up ever having his farm and be happy with what I did have.

Daddy stood, squared his shoulders, and looked out to sea as if there was something out there he'd lost. Daddy hadn't gotten everything he'd wanted either. I know he'd have cut off his right hand if it would have given him a few more years with Mamma.

I decided right then to show Daddy how much I appreciated having our own skiff. I decided to put thoughts of being a surfman out of my mind. I decided to become a very good fisherman.

The hunters had begun coming and going from Pea Island in November, around the same time as the ducks and geese had flown in from up north. Daddy said some of the hunters were rich men from the Northern states who came for sport, some were Southerners from the mainland who came for food, and still others came to try to earn their fortune from the Canada geese, brant, and ducks that flew so thick their flocks darkened the sky. The hunters stayed in the cabins up near Oregon Inlet but wandered the whole of Pea Island, and shots ringing out in the early morning, or any time of day, were a familiar sound.

One afternoon in January, the lifesavers were done with their drills and had gone off hunting or fishing, and Mr. Bowser was keeping watch on the lookout deck. I was sitting on a sand hill repairing our cast net, carefully tying knots with new line. I heard shotgun fire close by and thought nothing of it. Then I heard moaning and shouting. Two white men came stumbling out of the brush, one half carried by the other and trailing blood.

"There's the station!" one of the men cried. Then he spotted me and shouted, "You, boy, call the keeper. This man's been shot!"

I barged into the station and up the steps to the lookout deck.

"Mr. Bowser, hunters are here. One has been shot!" I cried.

Mr. Bowser used the spyglass to take one last good look at the calm seas, then followed me down the steps. We both hurried toward the hunters. The uninjured one was tall and sandy-haired. As we approached, he called, "Where's the keeper? We need the keeper."

"The keeper isn't here," Mr. Bowser said. "I'm the second in command. You'd better let me stop that bleeding—"

"Don't let that nigger touch me!" The injured man waved his

hands like he was shooing away gnats. He was stocky and bearded and looked like the older of the two. "You get me to a doctor, or the keeper, but I'm not having that nigger try to doctor me up!"

The man's right thigh looked like the flesh and trousers had been chopped up together in a meat grinder. Bird shot must be sprayed all through that leg, I thought.

"I can send Nathan, here, to find the keeper, but he's a colored man, too," said Mr. Bowser calmly.

A circle of blood had soaked into the sand under the injured man's right foot.

"Good God, you're bleeding to death! If you die, Mamma will never forgive me—let the boy doctor you, you idiot!" the sandy-haired man cried. He was almost as pale as his bleeding brother.

"Look who's calling me an idiot! It'll serve you right if Mamma never forgives you, shooting me like that."

"Help me get him inside." Mr. Bowser reached to support the bearded man.

"Get your hands off me!" he cried. But his face went suddenly slack, and his eyes rolled back. Then he snapped his head up and focused woozily on his brother. "I'm going. Tell Mamma I love her." His eyes rolled back again, his head fell sideways, and his body fell limp into his brother's and Mr. Bowser's strong arms.

"Oh God, he's dead!" the younger brother wailed.

"No, just stubborn and passed out cold from blood loss," said Mr. Bowser. "*Now* help me get him inside."

The three of us carried the bleeding man into the station. Mr. Bowser laid a piece of canvas over the messroom table, and we lifted him onto it. He sent me into the equipment room to fetch the medicine chest. By the time I returned, Mr. Bowser had cut the man's trouser leg to reveal a torn-up thigh with fat, muscle, and bird shot mixed in a gory mess.

"First we'll stop the bleeding, then I'll clean it some," said Mr. Bowser. "But you'll have to get him to Manteo to Doc Fearing, you understand?"

The younger brother nodded, his eyes wide with terror.

Mr. Bowser first tied a cord around the man's leg above the wound. "That's a tourniquet," he told me as he worked. "It will help stop the bleeding." Then he pressed with both his thumbs on a point below the man's groin. Slowly, blood stopped dripping from the wound. "Nathan, get the whiskey out of the medicine chest," he said.

He poured whiskey over the torn part of the leg and used tweezers to begin picking out the sprayed bird shot. The younger brother watched, his shoulders shaking with sobs.

"We spent all our money on a shad boat and barrels and ice," he said between sniffles. "We were going to sail back to Norfolk with five hundred birds—maybe a thousand." He used his sleeve to wipe snot from his nose. "The restaurants up north—Washington,

D.C., Baltimore, Philadelphia, New York—they're crazy for ducks and brant and geese. We were going to sell those birds and get rich and make Mamma proud." He broke down with a whole new round of sobbing. "But now look what I've done! I was behind him, and I tripped, and *bam*! Next thing I knew he was lying in his own blood, and . . ." He looked desperately at Mr. Bowser. "Can you save him?"

Mr. Bowser poured more whiskey over the wound, then poured a glass of it and handed it to the weeping man. "Pull yourself together. You're going to have to sail him to Manteo. Is your shad boat moored sound side?"

"Yes," said the man.

"You get him to Doc Fearing right away. He'll want to sew this leg up and keep a watch for lockjaw and infection."

Mr. Bowser poured a second glass of whiskey and handed it to me. "This rascal is going to wake up soon. When he does, pour that down his throat. It'll help with the pain and distract him from the fact that a colored man is patching up his leg." Mr. Bowser tore a piece of clean white linen and began to wrap it around the leg.

When the man woke up, he was too weak to yell at Mr. Bowser. I held the whiskey to his lips so he could drink it.

Mr. Bowser sent me to the stables for a wheelbarrow and some hay. We loaded the hunter into the wheelbarrow on a bed of hay and wheeled him over sound side to their shad boat. The younger brother thanked us over and over again.

"You get him to Doc Fearing now, you hear?" Mr. Bowser ordered.

The injured man was either too weak, too drunk, or too stubborn to say thank you.

When they'd left, Mr. Bowser shook his head. "Damn idiot. Would rather bleed to death than get help from a black man." Then he looked at me and searched my face. "You okay? All that blood didn't make you want to faint or gag or anything?"

"No, sir," I answered. It hadn't bothered me at all. In fact, it had been about the most interesting thing I'd ever seen.

"That's good," he said. He put his arm around my shoulders and we headed back to the station.

SIX

I stopped watching the surfmen do their drills and began spending each day with Daddy in the fishing skiff. Because it was winter, the fish in the sound weren't running much, so we spent a lot of our time talking about our small catch and wagering how big the catches would be when the weather turned warmer.

In the quiet, while we trawled along, Daddy told me stories about him and Mamma when they first met. He said he never thought a schoolteacher from a free family would take a second look at a fisherman who'd been born a slave and hardly had any schooling. But she had. He said Mamma used to laugh and say, "Must have been those strong arms of yours that got my attention, George, because it certainly wasn't the minnows hiding in your breeches cuffs that attracted me!" Daddy looked happy when he talked about her, with the sun shining on his smooth cheeks. And I liked hearing stories about Mamma, like she wasn't so far away. Daddy said the muscles in my arms looked bigger from hauling in the nets and rowing the skiff on windless days. He said he was proud of me.

On the night of January 12, the *James Woodall* ran aground. The surfmen didn't come to get us, which was just as well because helping with a rescue would have only made it harder for me to get surfman dreams out of my head. I liked hearing the story, though. The wreck happened near the New Inlet station, so the Pea Island crew went to help out the New Inlet crew. Mr. Etheridge said the surfmen from the Chicamacomico station came, too, with their new self-bailing, self-righting lifeboat, a huge boat that could fit twenty men in it. He said the surf was breaking all the way from the beach to the wreck, three hundred yards out, and that it took the strength of ten surfmen rowing like mad to keep that big lifeboat from being smashed against the wreck, even on its leeward side. They picked up all ten sailors and made it back to shore safely.

Besides fishing, the other thing I let myself think about was the way Mr. Bowser had fixed up that hunter's leg—stopped the bleeding and all. One afternoon when the station was empty, I went in and looked over the surfmen's collection of books to see if I could find the one that had taught Mr. Bowser to doctor that way. In the 1893 *Annual Report*, I opened to "Directions for Restoring the Apparently Drowned." There was a picture of a surfman kneeling over a man who looked half dead, pushing on his back. "Rule II. To expel water, etc., from the stomach and chest . . . ," I read. "If the jaws are clinched, separate them, and keep the mouth open by placing between the teeth a cork or small bit of wood; turn the patient on the face. . . ." Boy, did that sound familiar. I remembered the day they'd used me as the "apparently drowned" victim.

I scanned the bookshelf again and found a small brown volume: *Accidents and Emergencies: A Manual of the Treatment of Surgical and Other Injuries in the Absence of a Physician*. I pulled it from the shelf. Inside I found pictures showing where to press to stop bleeding in arms and legs, and a drawing of a tourniquet tied just above a man's elbow. This was it!

Suddenly I heard voices outside—the surfmen returning from hunting. I couldn't let them catch me snooping around! I slipped out the door and scrambled under the station between the pilings that held it up off the sand. I watched the surfmen's legs and feet as they walked, laughing and joking, toward the front door. Their voices faded as they went inside.

My heart pounded in my ears. The two books were still in my hands.

I hadn't meant to steal them. Actually, I'd only borrowed them, because I would certainly return them once I'd learned everything in them. I just needed a chance to read without anyone asking me why I was more interested in broken bones and dislocated shoulders than fishing and hunting like normal boys, or tease me about looking for naked pictures just because there happened to be one in *Accidents and Emergencies* that showed the location of the principal blood vessels in the body, or tell me I wasn't allowed because these weren't books for children. I wanted to read them in peace and quiet, and the only place I figured I could do that was in my hiding place under the station.

I decided I could read a little each day, and once I'd learned all I could, I would return them the first chance I got. I hoped the surfmen wouldn't notice the books were gone. They usually spent their time reading the newspapers and the fat novels that lined the bookshelves.

I read for a while about bone fractures and how to splint them. "In fracture of the jaw," I read, "close the mouth and put a bandage round, so as to keep the two rows of teeth against each other." The man in the drawing looked like those bandages were going to make it powerful hard to eat, talk, or even spit properly.

When I'd read about all I could put in my head for one day, I dug a shallow hole. I buried both books and marked the place with a mound of sand. I'd come back later with rags to wrap them in to protect them. Then I crawled out from between the pilings and ran home.

Every day I found time to sneak under the station to read. I read about cleaning and bandaging wounds and how to tell if a wound is infected. I learned the procedure for hypothermia: get the patient's wet clothes off, then rub his arms and legs with linseed oil, wrap him in blankets, and feed him a tablespoonful of hot water and whiskey every hour. I worked on memorizing the three pages in the *Annual Report* on resuscitating the apparently drowned. Mr. Meekins had told me that Keeper Etheridge sometimes woke the men up in the middle of the night and had them recite those pages just to make sure they really knew it. I figured if it was that important, there was no reason I couldn't memorize it, too.

Those books were the best thing I'd ever read—even better than *The Water World*, a book all about the ocean which my teacher, Miss Ella Midgett, loaned to me because she said I was such a good reader. And they gave me something to think about other than repairing nets, hauling in fish, mixing up brine for the fish barrels, and carting the barrels to Manteo to sell.

The best part about fishing was the visits every few days to Roanoke Island. Usually, all I had to do was help Daddy dock the skiff and carry the haul up to Griffin, Sample & Company General Store. Then Daddy wanted to be left alone to haggle over price with Mr. Griffin, so I was free to go find my friends. William and Floyd had been avoiding me since our fight in the boat room, so Fannie was who I usually set out to find.

If she didn't come running down to the dock to greet me, then I could find her in her backyard hanging clothes for her mother or inside doing some other household chore. The day

I found her chopping potatoes was the day I let her in on my secret.

"Pump me some cooking water, Nathan?" she asked, wiping her hands on her apron and eyeing the pile of sweet potatoes on the table.

She handed me a large pot, and I went out back to the pump. The water flowed ice cold and clear—much nicer than the rainwater off the roof we always used.

"That's a lot of sweet potatoes," I said when I came back in.

"Mamma wants four pies to bring to church tomorrow," she said, and started in on that pile with a peeler and a butcher knife like she was racing to some kind of sweet potato pie finish line.

I sat and watched the knife flash in her hand. Later, I wished I'd told her to slow down. It flashed and thwacked the cutting board, and flashed again until suddenly Fannie cried out and there was blood all over the board. She shook her cut hand and whimpered.

"Hold still," I told her. I stuck the dishrag into the pot of cold water, then grasped her hand with it and held it above her head. I squeezed the veins in her wrist with one hand and pressed the cold rag against the cut with the other. "This will stop the bleeding," I said. "You'll be fine."

There were beads of perspiration across her nose and cheeks, and she looked dizzy.

"Are you going to faint?" I asked. "Fainting usually makes the bleeding stop sooner, but I'd rather you didn't."

She scowled at me. "No, I am *not* going to faint."

"Well, if you feel like you're going to, just lower your head—"

"I told you I am not going to faint!" she snapped. She did look better now that she'd started arguing with me. "And I want to know how it is you know so much about fainting and cuts and the like." She stared me down the way Mamma used to when she was fixing to get the truth out of me.

"I . . . uh . . . I just know, I guess," I stammered.

If I hadn't been holding her hand up in the air, Fannie would have crossed her arms right then. As it was, she looked me up and down and said, "Miss Ella did not teach us that in school, and nobody is born knowing how to doctor, and you'd better give me a better answer than 'I just know.'"

I sighed. I could see that Fannie was at least as good as Mamma had been at getting to the truth. "You promise you won't tell anyone?" I pleaded.

Fannie nodded solemnly and made a cross over her heart with her free hand.

I lowered her hand and peeked at the cut. It wasn't that deep, and the bleeding had mostly stopped. I dipped a clean corner of the dishrag into the cold water again. "Here, hold this tight for a while longer," I said.

She looked at her cut, made a scrunched-up face, and quickly covered it with the rag.

I cleared my throat and leaned toward her. "I borrowed two

books on doctoring from the station library," I said, my voice low. "I've been studying them."

Fannie's eyes sparkled. "So *that's* how you knew!" she exclaimed. Then she sucked in her breath, as if she'd just that moment understood the part about "borrowing." "I bet you're whispering because the surfmen don't know that you took the books, right?"

I felt my face flush. "It was sort of an accident—and then once I had them, I didn't want to give them back before I read them."

This time Fannie did cross her arms over her chest. "Nathan Williams, I don't know whether to be proud of you or ashamed of you."

"Me neither," I admitted. "But I'm almost done with my studying. Soon I'll put them back where I found them, and no one will know, I promise."

She smiled. "And if you hadn't studied, I might still be bleeding all over those sweet potatoes! I promise I won't tell."

I bandaged Fannie's hand with a clean rag from her mamma's rag basket and helped her clean up the blood. Then Fannie supervised while I peeled and chopped sweet potatoes *slowly*.

If only I'd been able to keep my promise to Fannie the way she kept her promise to me.

SEVEN

February started out warmer than January had been. But on February 5, Mr. Moore from the weather station in Washington, D.C., telegraphed to Mr. Etheridge that we were about to be hit by a storm. Daddy and Grandpa and I moored our skiff on four long mooring poles, brought food and water inside the cabin, and waited.

The southeast gale started on February 6. It shook the cabin and beat the windows with rain and sand. We stuffed rags in the wall cracks, but we still had sand blow in during the dry spells and rain blow in during the wet spells. We used the chamber pot instead of the privy, and I got sick of the smell.

Daddy kept the fish-oil lamp lit and read to us from the *Fisherman and Farmer* newspaper. Even though it was two weeks old, it was better than listening to nothing but the clattering of the walls and roof. Grandpa pulled out his greasy deck of cards, and we played poker, using raw beans to bet with. Grandpa ended up with the most beans.

By the third day of the gale, I was weary from the constant clattering and shaking. We'd run out of meat, and the chamber pot was very much in need of emptying. During a dry spell, Daddy said he'd take care of the chamber pot and I'd go to the smokehouse for a goose. Over supper, we'd say a prayer that the gale would end.

I stuffed a sack under my shirt and pushed open the cabin door. If the door hadn't been built on the west side, I don't think I could have opened it. As soon as I stepped around the corner, the wind slapped me in the back and nearly toppled me over. The low-growing cedars looked like they were wrestling each other, and even the thick gray clouds had been swirled into spirals by the wind.

I plodded to the smokehouse, crouching low to keep my footing. Inside, the walls shook and creaked, and the smell of smoked meat and fish made my mouth water. I lifted a large goose off its hook and stuffed it into the sack.

Outside again, I faced the wind head on. Sand stung my cheeks and stuck in my eyes. It was hard to breathe. I held one hand over my face and, pressing my shoulders against the force of the wind, trudged to the cabin.

I slammed the door against the storm and tried to blink the

sand out of my eyes. There was sand in my mouth, and it crunched between my teeth.

"I hope this goose lasts until the gale ends," I said.

"I'd like the gale to end *now,* so we can eat that goose in peace and quiet," said Grandpa.

Daddy agreed.

By the fourth day the wind died some, and by the fifth day it was time for us to start digging out. Sand was piled up against the smokehouse, cabin, and privy. Our rain barrel was overflowing with fresh water but half buried in sand. We also had company. A herd of cows, confused by the storm, had decided that our yard was their new grazing area.

"I'll be planting my garden soon," said Grandpa. "I don't want those cows knocking down my fence and trampling my collards."

He told me to take a stick and shoo them away. I picked up Daddy's shotgun and aimed at one of the cows.

"I said *shoo* them, not shoot them," Grandpa said.

"I will," I said. I made a gunshot noise with my mouth, and took aim at another cow.

Grandpa leaned on his shovel and looked at me crossly. "You get yourself a stick and chase them away before I take a stick to *you.*"

I put down the shotgun. "Can't we shoot *one?*" I asked. "A scrawny one that'll die before spring anyway?"

Grandpa's cheek twitched. "You go shooting other people's cattle, you'll see where it gets you," he said.

I picked up a stick and went after the cows. They belonged to a rich white man who lived on the mainland. Pea Island was free grazing land, and he'd dropped them off here to graze on salt grass and anything else they could find. He'd pick them up next summer after they'd fattened up. The problem was, some of them wouldn't make it through the winter, with its storms and cold weather. I thought picking off one of the weak ones before it died and having us a nice steak would be a fine idea. Grandpa and Daddy didn't agree.

When we were done digging out at our house, Daddy said we should take our shovels over to the station to help. We found the crew digging out the stables, cookhouse, storage house, and station house. Mr. Wise called "Hello" to us from the roof of the station, where he was doing repairs.

Daddy, Grandpa, and I fell to work on digging out the cookhouse with Mr. Etheridge.

"We had a storm that hit around this same time in February last year," said Mr. Etheridge as he worked alongside us. The shovels made a nice clinking noise against the sand. "But last year's was worse—freezing weather, with snow and a terrible wreck up off the coast of Long Island, New York, where they lost almost the whole crew." A worried look crossed his face. "They'll be telegraphing soon to let us know of any casualties from this storm."

He and Daddy and Grandpa talked as they worked, but I stopped digging and stared at the mounds of sand piled up above the pilings of the station house. My stomach twisted into a knot. How on earth would I ever find the books again?

At suppertime, Mr. Etheridge invited us to stay. After four days of being cooped up, we all needed some company.

I went to the cookhouse to help Mr. Wescott chop turnips, carrots, and salt pork for stew.

"What do you think of this?" Mr. Wescott asked. He slapped a worn photograph onto the table next to me.

It was a three-masted schooner with her sails cut away, her rigging shiny with what looked to be a coating of ice, and her hull sunk so low that stormy waves washed over it.

"It's the wreck of the *Louis V. Place*," he said. "Happened up near New York in last February's storm."

I examined the broken ship. "Is that the one Mr. Etheridge told us about where most of the crew died?" I asked.

Mr. Wescott nodded. "That's the one." Then he asked, "Do you see anything strange in the picture? Look close."

I studied the ice-encrusted lines, the heavy storm-driven waves, the sails hanging low. Then, at the base of the starboard mast, I saw it. My hands went clammy. I shuddered. It was the ghostly face and shoulders of a man, twenty times its normal size.

"That's Captain Squires, the dead captain of the ship," Mr. Wescott said. "Come back to haunt it."

The skin on my back prickled. I stared at the mustached face with its captain's hat, floating disembodied in the rigging.

"Sailor from New York sold that photograph to me," said Mr. Wescott. "Said the one survivor—Stevens, I think his name was—goes door to door selling them."

I swallowed hard. "Why didn't they get rescued?" I asked.

"The crews from three stations—Blue Point, Lone Hill, and Point of Woods—tried for hours. They shot the line for the breeches buoy, but the sailors were so frozen and weak they couldn't tie it off. The surfboat was useless because the sea was full of porridge ice. The sailors climbed into the rigging, and I heard it told that through the night, one by one, they just got tired and dropped into the sea."

"What about Stevens?" I asked. "How did he get ashore?"

"Seems there were two—Nelson and Stevens—who hung on to the rigging together, and all night, to keep from freezing, they punched each other. The next day, when the storm finally died down just a bit, the lifesavers got the surfboat out to pick up the two. Their faces were swollen from the punches, but they were alive."

"But you said Stevens was the only survivor," I said.

"Nelson's feet were frozen solid. They sent him to the hospital on Staten Island to have them amputated, and he died of lockjaw a month later."

I nodded and looked down at the photograph again. "The captain didn't want to leave his ship," I said.

"I think you're right," said Mr. Wescott. "I heard he was one of the first to drop off the rigging. Probably felt like he'd abandoned his crew."

As we finished chopping the vegetables and meat, I wondered where the captain went when the *Louis V. Place* finally broke to pieces in the sea. I wondered where the other dead sailors went—did they come back to the ship, too? And I wondered where Mamma went when she closed her eyes and stopped breathing and Doc Fearing pulled the sheet up over her face.

Within a few days, Mr. Etheridge got the telegraph message he feared he would. The storm had caused a wreck—the *Alianza*—near Newburyport, Massachusetts. She was an old ship, and in the wild storm she broke to pieces in no time and her crew was thrown into the sea. Four of them swam to shore. The three that washed up dead looked like they'd been bashed and killed by the floating wreckage before they'd even had a chance to drown. They found the captain's body with the back of his skull caved in.

I was glad we hadn't had anybody die in a wreck on Pea Island. That would be like fighting a battle against the sea and losing. And I had my own small battle to fight now. It was me against the piles of sand that had built up under the station and buried the two doctoring books so deep I didn't think I'd ever find them.

EIGHT

Digging sand under a building on your hands and knees is nasty work. I got sand in my hair, down my shirt, and in the cuffs of my breeches. I got sweaty and sand stuck to my skin. And still, after two days of digging, I hadn't yet found the doctoring books. All I kept finding was planks of charred wood.

At first I thought a piece of old half-burnt firewood had blown under the station during the storm. Then I found another piece, and then a charred board that looked like it had been part of the wall of a house. It was much too big for firewood. And there was too much of it to have all blown under there. But what was it? How did it get there? Nobody in their right mind would build a fire under the station.

The more wood I found, the more curious I became, until I nearly forgot about the books and started digging for more charred wood instead.

So, it was almost by accident that my fingers finally touched the rags I'd wrapped the books in. The rags were soggy, and those books were a sight—all warped from the damp sand. I tried to wipe them dry with my shirt, but it was hopeless. I groaned out loud. When the surfmen found out, they'd probably ban me from the station.

I walked into the empty station house. Sunlight streamed through the salt-spray-covered windows. Quietly, I slid the books back onto the shelf. All I could do was wait to see what my punishment would be.

The next day, Daddy sent me to the station to borrow some saltwater soap because we'd run out and we were fixing to take our dirty clothes over sound side to wash them. Mr. Bowser fetched me the soap, and when he handed it to me, he said, "I see you're finally done with the books you borrowed. Did you learn something?"

My answer got stuck in my throat. I stood there with my mouth gaping open.

Mr. Bowser looked down at me, calm as anything, and said, "You tell your daddy I want you to walk the nine-to-midnight patrol with me tonight."

Somehow I closed my sagging mouth. "Yes, sir," I whispered, and took off out of there like I was being chased.

I told Daddy about walking the patrol, which he said would be fine, but I didn't tell him about the books or about the fact that Mr. Bowser was going to whip me good before we did any patrolling.

That night after supper and after I helped Grandpa wash the dishes and pans, I walked slowly to the station. I wasn't sure what I was going to say to Mr. Bowser, except to apologize for what I had done.

At the station, the men were still cleaning up after supper, each man washing his own dish in the cookhouse sink. Mr. Bowser said we'd start the patrol shortly and for me to wait in the station. He didn't seem awfully angry, and I counted that in my favor.

Just before nine o'clock, Mr. Bowser checked what he needed for the patrol: a lantern, Coston flares, his badge to exchange with the surfman from Oregon Inlet when they met, and a spyglass.

Dorman Pugh was getting ready to walk the south patrol. He packed the same items as Mr. Bowser did, except he brought the patrol clock for the key post box at New Inlet because no surfman would meet him there. He would turn the key, kept in the key post box, in the patrol clock to show that he'd walked the beat.

Mr. Bowser and I walked north along the shore toward Oregon Inlet. The moon caught the white foam of the breakers and made them shine.

"There's not likely to be any trouble tonight," said Mr. Bowser. "Calm seas, calm wind."

I trotted along beside him to keep up with his long strides.

"I've walked this patrol in wind so strong I could barely keep on my feet," said Mr. Bowser. "In fact, one night a gust swept my legs clear out from under me, and I landed on my back."

I nodded. I was still afraid to say anything much, still waiting for a whipping or at least a good talking-to.

"All right, boy," he said after we'd walked a while. "Directions for Restoring the Apparently Drowned. Let me hear it."

My eyes widened. How could he know I'd memorized it? I took a deep breath and started in, "Rule One. Arouse the patient. Unless in danger of freezing, do not move the patient, but instantly expose the face to a current of fresh air, wipe dry the mouth and nostrils, rip the clothing so as to expose the chest and waist, and give two or three quick, smarting slaps on the stomach and chest with the open hand. . . ."

"Good," he said when I'd finished. "What about fractures? Say a sailor gets brought in and his leg is broken. What are you going to do?"

"Is the bone sticking out or not?" I asked.

Mr. Bowser raised his eyebrows like he was impressed. "Not," he said.

"All right. Then cold compresses to keep the swelling down, and splint it with something like shingles or a board, or to the other leg if we can't find anything for a splint."

Mr. Bowser nodded. "Very good," he said.

He asked me more questions about hypothermia, heat exhaustion, head injuries from being hit with floating debris, how much whiskey you give a child and how much you give an adult. Apparently, I got most of the answers right.

"Now," Mr. Bowser said sharply, "tell me where you kept those books—in the bottom of your privy? Didn't anyone ever teach you how to take care of a book?"

My face flushed hot with shame. Of course someone had taught me. Mamma had loved books. "Mr. Bowser, I am sorely sorry about what I did," I said in a strong voice, just like I'd practiced it in my mind a hundred times. "I—" but before I could say more, Mr. Bowser interrupted me.

"Here's what I want in payment," he said. "When some of these wrecks come in, it's all we can do to keep up with the rescue, let alone treat all the men who are wounded and freezing and the like. You've got a good strong stomach for blood and gore, and you studied well. If I need you, I want you to help, you understand?"

"Help with . . . wounded sailors?" I asked, amazed.

"That's right," he said. "*If* I need you. Otherwise, you stay out of the way. Understood?"

I squared my shoulders. "Understood," I said. It was the proudest I'd ever felt.

Mr. Bowser lifted the spyglass to his eye and searched the horizon. So far we had sighted a schooner and two steamers. "All calm," he said.

As we walked, Mr. Bowser told me about what it was like

to walk this patrol during the worst storms and coldest weather. "Sometimes the north wind blows so hard the sand looks like thick fog along the ground. It stings your face and eyes so bad you have to walk sideways and backward part of the time just to make it," he said. "But the most unsettling thing isn't the bad weather. It's the time, say on the midnight-to-three-A.M. patrol, when you come upon a dead body all torn up and bloated from floating in the sea for days. It may only happen to you once, but let me tell you, you don't *ever* forget it."

That made my stomach do a flip-flop. And I watched where I put my feet after that.

At the north end of the patrol, he motioned me to sit with him next to a pile of old salvage wood. "This is where we meet the man on patrol from Oregon Inlet," he said. "Used to be we had a nice hut here, a halfway house, where we could get in out of the wind and rain." He patted one of the salvage boards. "But the Life-Saving Service thought that was too soft for us surfmen and tore all the huts down." He sniffed. "They sit in their warm offices up in Washington, D.C., and make decisions like that, you know."

Before long, Mr. Forbes from Oregon Inlet came walking down the beach. We all said hello, and he and Mr. Bowser shared information about the patrol so far, the boats they'd sighted and that there were no problems. They exchanged their badges to show they had met.

I was cold from sitting and glad to start walking south again. The pile of salvage wood made me think to ask Mr. Bowser about the charred wood under the station. Maybe he knew the answer to the mystery.

"Mr. Bowser," I began as he stood scanning the horizon with the spyglass.

"Damn," he said under his breath.

I was about to apologize for distracting him when I realized it wasn't me he was cursing at.

"See that schooner?" he demanded.

"Sure," I said. "She's so close I could about spit on her."

"Exactly," he said. "She's so close she's liable to hit a shoal." The schooner's hull was a dark mass, and her sails glowed white in the moonlight.

He pulled two Coston flares out of his satchel and gave me one to hold. "If the captain doesn't see the first one, we'll light the second."

In one quick motion, he pushed up against the bottom of the flare and it burst into a bright red flame. He held the light above his head and waved it.

"Turn offshore," he said, as if the flare could carry his words as well. "You're too close."

Moments later, we saw the schooner shift course and head out to sea. I let out my breath, relieved.

Mr. Bowser took the flare I'd been holding and put it back in his satchel. "They've probably saved thousands of lives, these flares," he said. "It surprises a lot of folks to find out they were invented by a woman."

"A *woman?*" I asked. I *was* surprised.

"Sure enough," he said. "Woman by the name of Mrs. Martha Coston. It was back before the war. She finished the work her husband started before he died."

The schooner was well out to sea now, and I decided to try my question again.

"Mr. Bowser, I was digging under the station and . . . there's a powerful lot of charred wood under there."

Mr. Bowser nodded. "I reckon there would be," he said. "They couldn't use the burned pieces when they rebuilt the station, so they just let them lie."

I frowned. "When they rebuilt the station?" I echoed.

"Right. After the fire." He gave me a sideways glance. "Nobody told you about the big welcome the white folks gave Mr. Etheridge when he became keeper?"

I shook my head.

"Burned the station to the ground, they did," he said, then spat onto the sand.

When he saw the scared look on my face, he added. "It was after everyone had gone home for the summer. They didn't mean to hurt anyone—just express an opinion."

I was only a little relieved. "Do they know who did it?" I asked.

"It was never investigated, and nobody was ever charged with the crime. You know how it is when a white man wrongs a black man—the authorities just look the other way like it didn't happen." He scuffed the sand with his heels as we walked along. "We've got a pretty good idea who it was, though. Three surfmen from another station who thought one of them should have been made keeper instead of Mr. Etheridge. But that was a good fifteen or sixteen years ago, and all three have been civil since then, so I won't name names and go digging up old hurts."

I nodded. I'd rather not know anyway.

We walked in silence for a while. The moon had risen high, and it glittered on the waves. I was getting sleepy.

It was nearly midnight when we traipsed up the ramp into the station. Mr. Bowser handed over the Coston flare and spyglass to Mr. Irving, who would walk the midnight-to-three-A.M. patrol.

They asked me if I could find my way home in the dark, and I told them I could. I stumbled, yawning, through the brush to our cabin and collapsed in bed next to Grandpa.

Grandpa and Daddy were both sound asleep, their breathing deep and rhythmic. I wanted to tell them about the patrol, but I didn't dare wake either of them. Still, I felt like I'd burst if I didn't tell someone. So I decided to tell Mamma. That's the way I fell asleep—talking to Mamma in the dark, telling her how even if I couldn't become a surfman, I already knew more than any of the boys on Roanoke Island about walking patrols, pulling the surfboat and beach cart to rescues, and taking care of wounded sailors.

NINE

If my wanting to become a surfman was like a fire I'd managed to mostly put out, then walking the patrol with Mr. Bowser was like a flame that lit it all up again. After that night I couldn't hardly stop myself from thinking about it. And my mind started working to make it seem possible, too. What if William and Floyd and all the other colored boys on Roanoke Island decided that what they really wanted was jobs at the fish market in Wanchese so they could live with their families instead of out on Pea Island away from everything? What if Mr. Etheridge retired—his hair and beard were already white—and Mr. Bowser became keeper and needed me to be his right-hand man in doctoring the wounded sailors? I knew it was crazy, but I couldn't help thinking that way. I guess there are times when the whole world tells you that you have to be one way, and you go on ahead and be how you want to be, anyway.

I was still fishing with Daddy every day. One morning after a heavy rain, Daddy and I were bailing out our skiff when we spotted the government sloop *Alert* just north of us on the sound. The *Alert*, with Lieutenant Cantwell and Superintendent Morgan aboard, was a regular sight at Pea Island. They came about once a month to bring the men's pay, deliver equipment like paint and stove brushes, and inspect all the stations along the Outer Banks. But today, as I watched, I saw that the *Alert* was not sailing smoothly. She was struggling to keep on an even tack.

"Something's wrong," I said to Daddy.

He put down his bailing pail and stood up to look. The *Alert*'s sails luffed and snapped in the wind, but she didn't come about. Suddenly we saw the red burst of a Coston flare.

Before Daddy had finished saying, "Go get the surfmen," I was running through the marsh toward the station.

The crew was in the middle of practicing with the signal flags. I called out, "The *Alert* is in distress! She's just sent up a flare."

Mr. Etheridge said not to bother with the surfboat, that the fishing skiffs they had moored sound side would be enough. I ran ahead, hoping that our fishing skiff could be one of the rescue boats, especially since it was the only boat already bailed out.

By the time I reached the sound, Daddy already had the sails rigged.

"George, can you take me out there to see what the trouble is?" Mr. Etheridge asked Daddy.

"Exactly what I had in mind," said Daddy.

I was so excited I almost tripped over the mooring ropes. I helped Daddy push the boat off, then jumped in and took my place at the rudder. Daddy sheeted in the sails and we were on our way—me, Daddy, and Keeper Etheridge heading out to rescue the officials from Washington, D.C. If William or Floyd found out I was getting to do such a thing, I'd be in for another shiner for sure.

We sailed up alongside the *Alert* and luffed our sails.

"Lieutenant Cantwell, sir," Mr. Etheridge greeted a tall white man in uniform with a blond mustache and a grumpy look on his face.

"The damned rudder's become unshipped," said Mr. Cantwell. "She's gone out of control, and I've had to drop anchor."

Another, shorter white man, also in uniform, appeared along with several young men—members of the crew.

"Superintendent Morgan, sir," Mr. Etheridge addressed the shorter man. "I'm sorry to hear of the trouble."

Superintendent Morgan nodded. "We'll need nails and iron bolts to repair the rudder," he said. "And a place to stay until we can sail again."

Mr. Etheridge looked toward shore, where the crew was just starting out in a couple of fishing skiffs. "We'll have you and your crew back to the station in no time," he said.

The ship's crew lowered a ladder, and the two officers

climbed down and stepped carefully into our skiff. They took their seats, their backs ramrod straight as they sat on the rough wooden boards. I admired their uniforms: the deep blue of their coats, the gold glint of the buttons.

"Nathan." Daddy had to nudge me out of staring. "I still need you to man the rudder."

I blinked. I moved to the back of the skiff and closed my hand around the smooth handle of the rudder. As Daddy sheeted in the sails, we began to move easily over the water. Could this be real? Was I actually sailing Lieutenant Cantwell, Superintendent Morgan, and Keeper Etheridge back to shore in our boat? I had to bite my lip to keep from grinning and laughing out loud. And everyone had been telling me not to hope for things that seemed impossible!

We moved swiftly, the skiff slapping over the water, the wind in my face, and the morning sun lighting up the marsh grasses onshore. I decided then and there that I would never call anything impossible again.

TEN

The knocking at our door was loud and insistent, and it woke me from a deep sleep. Daddy roused himself to answer it. I listened to the news: there was a wreck, a three-masted schooner. One of the surfmen, George Midgett, was ill, and the Oregon Inlet crew had not yet arrived. The schooner had already begun to break up. They must launch the surfboat, but quickly. They needed our help—*now*.

I was out of bed by the time Daddy turned from the door. We threw on our clothes and ran through the brush to the station. A howling northwest wind blew sand in our faces. Bright stars twinkled in the black sky.

The surfboat had just been rolled down the ramp. Daddy and I immediately snatched up drag ropes to pull. The sand gave way under my feet, and I heard the wheels creak as we hauled the boat along the shore, south toward the dark hulk of the stranded schooner. The surf pounded, loud and jumbled.

When we reached the wreck, Mr. Etheridge shouted, "Unload!" Instead of standing out of the way with Daddy, I took what I figured to be Mr. Midgett's job of helping to lower the boat into the shore break. Then, with the shouting of "Take oars!" and "Go!," I pushed hard, running alongside the surfboat. I helped shove the boat through the pounding breakers until a cold wave washed over my head. I gulped in salt water and choked. Someone's strong hands grabbed my arms and hoisted me upward. I flopped over the side of the boat. It was now afloat and being rowed quickly out to sea.

"Damn you, Nathan!" It was Mr. Bowser's voice. But he was too busy rowing to say any more.

I choked on the water still in my lungs. A wave crashed over the side of the boat and drenched my face again. I blinked salt water away and saw an unmanned oar. I would prove I'd done the right thing. I would row as well as the other surfmen.

I set my oar to work in rhythm with the men. The boat rocked crazily, buffeted by the uneven waves. Pull . . . pull . . . I put my mind to the rowing, not the danger. Stripes of white foam glowed in the moonlight with inky black sea in between. Short bursts of my own breath sounded in my ears.

The schooner, dark and huge, loomed ahead. Excited shouting greeted us. We pulled the surfboat along her leeward side, being careful not to collide. One of the sailors on deck held a coil of rope. When we came near, he swung his arm back and cast the rope out, but a gust of wind took the rope and flung it into the ocean. It landed just off the side of the surfboat, hardly two feet out of my reach.

Now, I thought. Now I'll show them what I'm made of. Now I'll show them what a good surfman I'll become. I stretched my oar out into the water, caught a loop of the rope, and drew it closer. Then I leaned out and plunged my hand down. My fingers closed around the rough rope.

Someone shouted, "Nathan, no!" I felt a jolt, a moment of weightlessness as the surfboat catapulted me up. I hit the sea with a slap. Cold, dark water closed over my head.

I was still holding on to the rope. They can pull me up, I thought. Just don't let go.

I only caught a glimpse of it—large and black, tossing in the waves. It slammed into my head with blunt force. There was a flash of white-hot pain, then darkness.

Someone was rubbing my legs and feet. The pungent smell of linseed oil filled my nostrils and made my aching head hurt even worse. I tried to open my eyes but felt as if the lids were made of lead.

"He's coming to." That was Daddy's voice.

"Get some whiskey and hot water ready," I heard Mr. Etheridge say.

I felt the itchy wool blanket that was wrapped around me. Someone pulled it aside and began to rub my arms and hands. My muddled brain found the pattern and put the pieces together. Wrapped in a blanket. Arms and legs rubbed with linseed oil. Whiskey and hot water.

My mouth was dry and my tongue felt swollen. "Hypo . . ." I tried to talk, but it came out slurred. I swallowed, wet my tongue, and tried again. "Hypothermia," I said softly.

"What?" Daddy leaned close to hear. I could feel his breath on my cheek. "Speak up, Nathan."

"Hypothermia," I said more clearly. "That's what you're treating me for."

There was a moment when no one spoke, whoever was rubbing my limbs stopped rubbing, and the air in the room seemed to hold still. Then Mr. Bowser's voice shattered the silence.

"Good God, boy! Are you daft? You came near to dying on us, and your first words when you come back from death's door are straight from the medical manual?"

I still didn't open my eyes, but I heard their laughter—nervous, relieved laughter.

I'd had a firsthand demonstration of how those sailors in Massachusetts died: by being smashed in the head by floating debris. My head being so bashed up saved me from getting a whipping, but it didn't save me from being scolded, reprimanded, and reminded a hundred times that what I had done was very stupid, put the lives of the surfmen and sailors in danger, and had better not *ever* be done again. Daddy said, "This is the craziest thing you've ever done, boy. I've got a good mind to keep you away from the rescues altogether." Mr. Bowser said, "I told you to stay out of the way unless I needed your help. Don't you know how to stay out of the way?" And Mr. Etheridge said, "I thought you had better sense than that, Nathan. I'm disappointed in you." I think I would have rather gotten a whipping and not had to hear about my mistake over and over again.

Mr. Etheridge decided to keep me at the station. Even I knew there wasn't much to be done about a fractured skull. All the medical manual had said was "Place the patient on his back and apply cold, wet cloths to the head." But Mr. Etheridge wanted to keep a watch on me in case I took a turn for the worse, so I lay in bed at the station feeling miserable. My head hurt so bad I could barely move without my eyes watering. The bandage on my forehead, where the plank had hit me, had to be changed every day. I kept a cloth over my eyes because even a little sunlight sent shooting pain into my head. But the worst injury was to my spirit. I felt that just when I'd started to hope again, just when I'd begun to feel that the impossible might yet be possible, it had all come crashing in on me. Now I was so ashamed I wished I could shrivel up and disappear. I vowed that once I was well enough to return home, I would not show my face at the station ever again.

For three days I lay on my cot in the bunk room, listening to the voices of the sailors and surfmen downstairs as they played cards and told stories. I smelled the cigarette and pipe smoke as it wafted up the steps and heard the clinking of forks on plates during mealtimes. Mr. Wescott brought my meals up to me, though I didn't eat much and mostly drank water.

When the surfmen and sailors came up to the bunk room in the evenings, they asked how I was doing, and Mr. Bowser changed the bandage on my head. I answered their questions with as few words as possible, counting the minutes before they would settle in for the night. In the dark, I listened to their snoring and hoped that the next day would be the day I'd be well enough to go home and not have to face them anymore.

On the fourth day, I was surprised to hear a different voice when my breakfast was brought upstairs to me. "Sit up, Nathan. Take that rag off your face and look at me. I want to talk to you." It was Mr. Meekins.

I did as he said, wincing, as sitting up made the blood pound in my head. I squinted my eyes almost shut against the light, but I looked at him. His face was serious and a little bit angry. His straight nose and square jaw under the polished brim of his surfman's cap made him look very official.

"I think your pride is hurt worse than your head," he said.

I let my breath out in a slow stream. It was a relief to have someone name where my real pain was coming from. "Yes, sir," I said softly.

"There's no doubt you acted like a fool the other night," he said. "But I'm good and tired of you acting like a fool now. If there's anything to be learned from this, it's how to be a man. Accept that you made a mistake, say your apologies, decide you'll do it different next time, and stop sulking. If I see one more mopey look on your face, I'm liable to slap you upside the head—then we'll see which hurts worse, your pride or your head."

I cringed. "Yes, sir." I tried to say it with strength.

He stood to leave. "And eat your breakfast today." He waved one of his large hands at my tray of biscuits and fig preserves. "It better be gone when Mr. Wescott comes to get the tray."

He left me alone to sort out the things he'd said.

I know it takes courage to meet a storm head-on, but that day it felt like it took even more courage to meet my own foolishness head-on. First I apologized to Mr. Etheridge for jumping into the surfboat rather than simply helping to pull it. Then I apologized to Mr. Bowser for not staying out of the way when I should have. He punched my arm gently and said, "That's all right. But if you do it again, we'll throw you overboard." The sailors and surfmen laughed good-naturedly. I tried to smile and held my head to ease the throbbing the punch in the arm had caused.

When Daddy and Grandpa came to see how I was doing, I told them I was sorry for all the trouble I'd caused.

"You've left me to work on that garden fence all by my lonesome," Grandpa said. He patted my hands, and I could see worried creases around his eyes.

"I'll be okay, Grandpa," I assured him. "And I'll come help you with the fence soon. My head hurts a little less every day. Mr. Bowser said I probably have a crack in the skull, but it'll heal up in a couple of weeks."

Daddy shook his head. "A cracked skull. I should send you to live with Mamma's cousin Mabel before you get yourself killed out here."

"I've learned my lesson, I promise," I insisted. Living with Cousin Mabel, with her strict rules about cleanliness and manners, would be a very mean punishment.

Daddy eyed me carefully—my bandaged head, my squinted eyes, my arms skinny from little food and no work. "I suppose maybe you have," he said.

Within a couple of days, I was feeling good enough to sit up part of the day. Mr. Wescott said he was tired of carrying my food to me and it was time for me to join the men for supper downstairs. I gripped my head with one hand, the banister with the other, and walked slowly down the steps.

At the supper table, I got my first really good look at the sailors from the *Maggie J. Lawrence*. There were seven of them: two Yankees, two Southern men, a Swede, a Norwegian, and Mr. Abilgas from Manila. They had, I learned, sailed from

Philadelphia and were bound for Charleston, South Carolina, with a cargo of coal when they'd wrecked. They were still waiting for a steamer that would take them up to Norfolk but said they were happy to wait because here the company and the food were excellent. They said I'd missed lots of good stories, smoking, and card playing while I'd been lolling around in bed.

After supper, Mr. Abilgas said I hadn't missed everything because he'd saved his best story for me. He was a short man with a broad brown face and hooded eyes. He leaned back in his chair to begin his story.

"It happen at Hendricks Head Light, in Maine," he said, his dark eyes flashing. "During winter—a snowstorm! The waves—like monsters—ten, fifteen, twenty feet high." He looked around the group of us slowly. "The sea, cold like ice," he said in a sinister voice. "A big ship—a whaler—run aground." He smacked the heel of his hand against the table to show how the bottom of the ship hit the rocks. "The lighthouse keeper, he see the distress flag. But he all alone, only his wife, no rescue station.

"The keeper and his wife, they build a big bonfire." Mr. Abilgas raised his arms to show the hugeness of the fire. "Let people on ship know that somebody see them."

"Didn't they try to save them?" I blurted out. What good was a bonfire with no rescue on the way?

He shook his head. "No. Keeper has only a small dory.

Waves crashing too big, and snow filling the sky like a million white birds.

"But!" Mr. Abilgas fixed me with his eyes. "The keeper go to the shore to see what might be floating up.

"He see a big bundle, floating, tossing. He get a boat hook and run out in the waves. He reach to hook the bundle, and *paff*! A big wave throw him and bundle up onto the shore."

The men laughed, but my memory of being thrown in a similar way while reaching into the ocean was still too fresh for me to laugh.

"He look down at the bundle and say to himself, 'Dammit, I just rescue a featherbed!'"

The sailors and surfmen really laughed then, and even I cracked a smile.

Mr. Abilgas held up one finger. "Then he see that the featherbed tied to another featherbed—like there something inside. So he cut ropes and find a box."

By now I was leaning forward.

"And something inside box making sound like a cat."

My eyes widened.

"He open box, and do you know what he find inside?"

I shook my head.

"A baby."

"Naw!" Mr. Bowser slapped his leg in disbelief.

Mr. Abilgas nodded emphatically. "A baby girl—and she

crying, screaming. And the keeper's wife she yelling do this and do that, tell him take her inside she going to freeze, put more wood on fire, go milk cow in middle of night.

"The keeper's wife still have clothes for baby in house because her own baby die few months before. They get her warmed up, give her milk, soon she sleeping.

"The keeper go outside to signal to ship that baby safe now. But he see that ship gone—all broken up. Everybody dead."

We were silent.

"He look in box and find two blankets, locket, and note that say, 'Lord God, I commend my child into your hand.' It written in lady's writing—must be mother."

"What happened to the baby?" I asked.

"They keep her. She replacement for one they lost." He folded his hands over his round stomach and smiled.

"That happened up in Maine? For real?" Mr. Wescott asked.

Mr. Abilgas nodded. "Little girl grown up now. She happy, strong."

One of the other sailors broke in with a new story. "Did you hear about that life-saving crew up in Michigan on Lake Superior—Marquette station, I think it is—got a *bear* for a pet?"

Several of the surfmen snorted like they thought it was a joke.

"It's true," the sailor insisted. "Raised it from a cub, they did. It eats out of their hands—probably sits down to table with them!"

Everyone laughed, including me.

ELEVEN

The *Maggie J. Lawrence* broke up, and when pieces of her hull and cargo started floating in, the sailors and surfmen worked to pull them up onshore to get ready for the auction. My head was still bandaged and still ached like it was being hit with a sledge-hammer every time I moved too fast, so all I could do was sit on a sand hill to watch. They hitched the government team to the heavy slabs of wood and tangled masses of sail and rope and had the mules drag it all up onto dry sand, where the men could un-tangle it and sort it out. Mr. Etheridge got his ankle sprained leading the government team, and Mr. Bowser bandaged it so it wouldn't swell too bad, so after that he had to sit and watch, too.

The steamer finally came to carry the sailors up to Norfolk, where they could board the trains to go back home. Captain Holloway stayed at the Pea Island station to wait for the auction.

The day of the auction—or vendue, as lots of people called it—February 20, was bright and almost springtime-warm. In the morning, Daddy, Grandpa, and I went sound side to greet folks as they arrived. The sound was already dotted with skiffs, the morning sun lighting up white sails against blue sky and water. A steady southwest wind brought the boats skimming in to shore.

We helped drag boats up into the marsh, where they would stay put. There were white folks coming to buy and the surfmen's families coming to picnic, and a lot of people coming because this vendue was the most interesting thing going on today for miles around.

Daddy told me to help Mrs. Collins on account of she had three small children, two baskets full of ham, smoked fish, corn bread, apples, and jam, and about four blankets to lay everything out on. We carried it all over ocean side near the station house, where folks were gathering around the piles of salvage wood, rope, and sailcloth.

Fannie arrived not long after I'd gotten Mrs. Collins settled. She grabbed my hands and swung me around in a circle. "Look at that nasty old head bandage!" she exclaimed, laughing. "Seems to me you've been being the *patient* instead of doing the doctoring." Then her face fell. "Does it hurt?" she asked.

"Only when someone swings me in a circle," I answered.

She laughed again, then tipped her head close to mine. "I didn't tell anyone about your studying," she whispered.

"It's all right—Mr. Bowser knows. He even asked me to help him with wounded sailors," I said proudly.

She narrowed her eyes at me and smiled. "I *knew* it," she said.

"Knew what?" I asked.

But Seabright ran up and pulled on Fannie's arm. "Take me to pet the mules, Fannie," she whined. "You promised and William won't come with me and Mamma says I can't go alone."

Fannie waved to me as she let Seabright drag her away toward the stables.

Soon the auction began, with the Commissioner of Wrecks shouting out prices and people raising their hands to show what they were willing to pay. He sold everything off for Mr. Holloway, for a grand total of one hundred and sixty dollars and twenty cents.

After that was when folks started pulling food out of the baskets and the children started clamoring for the surfmen to set up the breeches buoy for rides. Mr. Etheridge handed me his pocket watch so I could time the crew's breeches-buoy drill. They dragged the beach cart out onto the white sand and got ready to start. When Mr. Etheridge shouted, "Action!" I started timing. The men raced to bury the sand anchor, aim the Lyle gun, fire the shot line, fasten the hawser line to the wreck pole, which took the place of the ship's mast during drills, raise the tall, X-shaped crotch, and haul the breeches buoy into place. The whole thing took four minutes and forty-five seconds.

Everyone applauded—the adults because the crew had done such an impressive job, and the children because they were excited about riding the breeches buoy.

"I want to ride first!" cried Seabright, and she ran to the wreck pole to climb up. Mr. Meekins steadied her as she climbed and helped her into the breeches buoy, where she sat grinning with her skinny brown legs and bloomers sticking out of the breeches. A group of children pulled on the whip line. Seabright squealed as the rope slid through the pulley and she was sent, dangling high in the air, from the wreck pole to the crotch. It was better than any carnival ride I'd ever seen.

Someone jabbed me in the ribs, and I turned to see Floyd, almost cross-eyed, getting a good look at my head bandage. William and Charles, another boy from school, were there too, and the three of them surrounded me, staring. I let my breath out in a slow stream, trying to stay calm. One light punch to the head would have blinded me with pain. I hoped the crowd, which included their own mothers and fathers, would keep them from starting a fight.

"I guess they won't be letting you help with rescues anymore," William said bluntly.

It hurt more than a blow to the head. I said nothing.

Floyd sniffed. "That bandage doesn't cover half his head," he said, obviously annoyed by the inaccuracy of the story he'd been told. "It's just a strip."

I could have told him that it used to be bigger and was smaller now that my wounds were healing up, but I didn't want to talk about any of it—especially not to these boys.

"Come on," said William, "let's go ride."

At that moment, from the direction of the wreck pole, came a loud squeal. When I looked, I saw Fannie trying to climb the pole and her mother pulling her down by her ankles.

"Why can't I ride?" Fannie cried, jumping to the ground.

"You get away from there!" Her mother, a large woman, was huffing from the effort of having pulled her daughter back to earth.

Fannie stood with her hands on her hips. "But Floyd gets to go, and I've always ridden, and—"

"Don't you sass me, and don't put your hands on your hips when you talk to me," her mother ordered.

Fannie dropped her hands and her eyes.

"You'll be turning thirteen in a few months, and you've got no business sitting in those breeches with your bloomers sticking out for all the world to see."

Floyd snickered as he pushed past Fannie and hoisted himself up the wreck pole. Fannie slapped at him and scowled.

"May I ride like some of the older girls do, then?" Fannie asked quietly. "I can sit on the buoy with my feet in the breeches."

Her mother lifted her hands toward the sky. "Lord have mercy! And fall to your death?" She took Fannie by the arm and pulled her away from the wreck pole. "You go lay out that blanket and set out that food and act like a lady."

Fannie's shoulders slumped as she walked over to her family's picnic basket. She didn't ask me to, but I followed and helped her lay out the blanket and plates of fried bluefish, corn bread, candied sweet potatoes, and a jar of fig preserves. There was a long wooden spoon for serving the sweet potatoes and a small silver spoon for the preserves.

She handed me a piece of corn bread and we sat together to eat. That's when I had an idea.

"It's your dress that's the problem," I said.

She gave me a sideways look. "What?"

"It's your dress and the breeches buoy. They don't go together. It's made for rescuing sailors, in *breeches*."

Fannie was looking at me like I wasn't making sense, and I was thinking of the pair of breeches I'd scrubbed clean the day before and hung in the sun to dry. They were neatly folded at the foot of my bed, in my cabin, just a few hundred yards away.

"So?" Fannie wiped corn bread crumbs from her lips.

"So, you want to borrow some breeches?" I asked.

Fannie caught her breath and covered her mouth with one hand. "Mamma would whip me so I wouldn't sit for a month!" she exclaimed.

I shook my head. "I don't want you to get in trouble. Forget I mentioned it."

But Fannie's eyes were gleaming. "Yes," she said, and looked at me expectantly.

"Yes?" Now I was confused.

"Yes, I would like to borrow some breeches," she said firmly. She stood and reached down to help me up.

We walked through the brush to my cabin. I told her where the breeches were and waited outside while she dressed. When she came outside to show me, she spun around. The breeches were completely hidden under her dress.

"No one will even suspect," she said triumphantly.

"Not until you ride," I said, raising one eyebrow.

"That doesn't matter," she said, and flounced ahead of me as we walked back to the picnic.

When we got there, William was riding the buoy, hooting as he swung through the air.

"We've got to make sure Mamma doesn't catch me while I climb up," she whispered.

I studied the situation. Mr. Meekins was still helping children climb up the pole. Most of the adults were standing or sitting in groups, talking and eating, and children were taking turns pulling on the whip line to make the breeches-buoy ride work. Fannie's mother was chatting and laughing with several other women.

"I'll help you," I said. "Let's go *now*."

We ran to the wreck pole, and I shoved Fannie in front of me toward it.

"Miss Fannie," Mr. Meekins began to scold, "didn't your mamma—"

"I've got breeches on," Fannie interrupted, and swished up her skirts to show him.

While Mr. Meekins was still too surprised to stop us, I pushed Fannie up the pole and climbed up behind her so no one could grab her ankles. She reached the top and hoisted herself into the buoy. She gave me a huge grin as she dangled there, her breeches-clad legs sticking out, waiting for the children to pull on the rope.

But the breeches buoy didn't move. Fannie's grin faded.

"Mamma doesn't want her riding." It was Floyd's voice. He had hold of the whip line and was refusing to let anyone pull it.

Fannie looked down at me, fear and disappointment on her face. Now she would get a whipping and wouldn't even get to ride.

A flash of anger set my head throbbing. I swung down off the pole and marched over to Floyd. "Your mamma didn't want her riding in a dress. She's wearing breeches now," I snapped. I yanked the whip line out of his hands and began to pull. Seabright took hold of the rope with me, and several of the other children did the same, and we sent Fannie swinging gently through the air.

Fannie smiled as she looked around, taking in the view on what might well be her last breeches-buoy ride. I imagined what she was seeing—vast ocean stretching out blue-green in the sunshine, long white shimmering beach, the tops of picnickers' heads, all her friends and family.

The commotion when the ride was over rivaled the wildest street arguments I'd ever seen in Elizabeth City: Fannie's mother yelling at Fannie for disobeying and smacking her on the rear with a wooden spoon, Floyd shouting that it was my fault for pulling on the rope, Fannie crying and trying to show her mother that she was wearing breeches, so she hadn't displayed her bloomers at all, and Fannie's father trying to calm everyone down so he could at least understand what was going on.

When Fannie had a chance to explain, it didn't make her mother or brother any less angry. Once my part in it was clear, Fannie's mother gave me several hard swats on the behind with the wooden spoon, which I sincerely hoped would make Floyd happy and give him less reason to punch me in the face at a later date.

Fannie's father sent me and Fannie back to my cabin to return the breeches. We walked in silence, Fannie still sniffling. I felt like I'd done a terrible thing—made a fool of myself again and gotten Fannie in a heap of trouble. I wished I'd never suggested the breeches in the first place. It was all my fault.

At the cabin, I slumped against the rain barrel while Fannie slipped quietly inside to change. When she came out, I tried to form the words. I still couldn't look at her, but I had to say I was sorry.

"Fannie, I—" I began.

But suddenly Fannie wrapped her arms around my neck and pressed her cheek against mine. "Nathan," she said into my ear, "that was the best ride *ever*!"

And before I was over being shocked and surprised, she kissed me on the cheek, then skipped on ahead back to the picnic.

TWELVE

After the night I got thrown out of the surfboat, I didn't ask if I'd be allowed to help with more rescues. I was afraid to find out the answer.

As it was, the rest of February and all of March passed without another wreck. By the time April came in with sunny days and steady southwest winds, Mr. Etheridge said if we were lucky, there wouldn't be any more wrecks this season. It's the winter storms and the way the shore gets steeper in the winter that cause the ships to run aground. He said the "active season" for the life-saving stations used to be December 1 to March 31: the heart of the winter. But in 1877, the U.S. warship *Huron* wrecked near Nags Head just a week before the active season was to begin, and with no one at the life-saving station to rescue them, ninety-eight men drowned. After that the government decided to make the active season longer, and these days it ran from August 1 to May 31—just in case.

The geese, ducks, and hunters all left, and the shad and blue-fish started running. Daddy and I were busy every day in the fishing skiff, and sometimes Grandpa came, too, because the nets got so heavy we needed his help.

On April 30, Lewis Wescott went home to Roanoke Island, because he was the "winter man" and only worked December to April. The ocean was still chilly, but I was wanting to start my swimming lessons. So, one day when the waves had whipped themselves up to at least five feet high, I presented myself to Mr. Meekins and asked if he would show me how to fight them.

Mr. Meekins laughed. "You don't fight them," he said. "You kind of sneak by while they're not looking."

The other surfmen laughed, too, and I felt like Mr. Meekins was making fun of me. A few minutes later, I found out he was just telling the truth.

He led me down to the shore, and we both took off our shirts and rolled up our breeches.

"The first trick is getting past the shore break," he said. "It'll try to grab you and topple you."

I nodded. I'd certainly had that happen lots of times.

"The water is cold, so you want to get in slowly and not have too much of a shock, right?" he said.

"Right," I said.

"Well, that's wrong," said Mr. Meekins. "You've got to run into the shore break, crash through it as fast as you can, and before it even sees you coming, you'll be out past it."

I shivered just thinking of it.

"Then, once you're in the waves, you probably think you ought to stay on top of them—keep your head above the water, stay where you can see the next one coming, right?"

I wasn't sure whether to agree or disagree this time, so I just waited.

"Well, that's wrong, too," said Mr. Meekins. "The top of the wave is where the power is. If you sneak *under* the power, the wave won't even know you're there. Then you pop your head up, spot the next one coming, and dive under it. You understand?"

I understood that I should do exactly the opposite of what made logical sense to me.

"Stay next to me, do what I do, and you'll be fine," he said.

He stared at the ocean for a moment, then shouted, "Go!" We ran full speed into the shore break, crashing through it and sending spray into the sunlit air. The cold took my breath away, and the waves sucked at my feet and legs, but I lifted them and kept running until I thrust myself into the deep water behind the break.

"Did it!" I cried between gasps for breath.

But there was no time to celebrate. A five-foot wave was towering over my head, ready to explode.

"*Under!*" Mr. Meekins yelled.

I dove. Water rumbled in my ears and I was rolled sideways. Salt water rushed up my nose. I felt the rough bottom against one hip, then, suddenly, I was floating. Mr. Meekins's words sounded in my mind. "Pop your head up, spot the next one. . . ." I gave one hard stroke toward the surface. I shot out stale breath, sucked in new air, took a split-second glance at the next monster wave, and dove under quickly.

On this wave I'd made it in time. My body curved in a graceful arc, down toward the bottom, then up to the surface. The turbulence washed over the soles of my feet as they flipped like fins behind me. The wave hadn't even known I was there!

Again, there was no time to relax, only a moment for a new breath and another dive toward the bottom. Over and over we dove, surfaced in the troughs, and dove again, working our way out, Mr. Meekins strong as a dolphin beside me. He was right. It wasn't fighting. It was sneaking.

We swam out through the breakers toward the horizon. Once, I got a faceful of foam and gulped in salt water and air until I was choking. Then, with a strong stroke of my arms, I swam past the last breaker. Here the green mountains of water rose and fell without tossing me. Mr. Meekins floated near me.

"Good swimming," he said.

"William and Floyd taught me to swim, off Roanoke Island," I said between quick breaths.

"They're good swimmers," he said. "A surfman's got to know how to swim, even through rough breakers. Never know when the surfboat might capsize."

"Right," I said.

We were far from shore now, with the white foam of the breakers separating us from land. I paddled with my hands and turned myself around. A wave lifted me up, and I spotted five gray fins gliding through the water nearby.

"When they see us, they'll come closer," said Mr. Meekins. "They're curious—think we're strange fish."

The dolphins swept close, then leapt out of the water, their sleek gray bodies glistening.

"I could almost touch them!" I shouted.

The dolphins circled us, then swam farther out to where a group of pelicans were swooping down and grabbing at something in the water.

"There's a school of fish out there," said Mr. Meekins. "Dinner for everyone."

The excitement of the dolphins left me panting, out of breath.

"You tired?" Mr. Meekins asked.

"No," I answered, and we kept on swimming.

But soon my arms and legs felt like limp rags. I knew I'd best get in before I had no strength left.

"Now I'm tired," I said.

"We'll swim back into the breakers and ride one in," said Mr. Meekins.

Ride? I gave him a worried glance. No one had said anything about riding.

We swam together back toward shore. When we passed the breaker line, I felt the sucking that comes before a wave topples. I spun around quickly and dove under, as we'd done on our way out. When I popped my head up, Mr. Meekins was gone.

My chest tightened. My arms felt suddenly weaker. Ride? I forgot to dive. The wave took my body. It tumbled me over, rolling me sideways and head over heels. When it let me loose and rolled past, I was closer to shore, but still amid the breakers. Before I could catch my breath and dive under, the next wave grabbed me and tossed me toward shore in a rolling heap. Water shot up my nose. The wave shoved me against the rough bottom. I felt sand under my knees and scrambled to my feet. I took two lurching steps forward, crumpled as the wave sucked backward, then fell on my face as the next wave pushed me from behind.

I managed to crawl to shore. There, I crouched, gasping and heaving, spitting out salt water and sand, feeling the sting of scrapes on my back, arms, and knees.

Mr. Meekins stood and looked down at me. "You could have ridden in a little better, but other than that you did fine," he said.

I suggested that riding waves be part of our next swimming lesson, and he agreed.

THIRTEEN

George Midgett got weaker instead of stronger, with a loud cough and pains in his chest, so he was sent home to Roanoke Island to have a good rest. We thought he'd come back in a while to finish out the season, but he never did. Mr. Tillett came as his substitute, the way he'd done for Mr. Pugh when he was on leave last winter to get married.

The last few weeks before the crew left for the summer, I helped them overhaul the life-saving equipment, whitewash the stable and storehouse, oil the wood inside the station, paint the lifeboat and the window sashes, and pack up all their belongings in preparation for going home. They were happy to be going to live with their families for two whole months. I was sorry to see them go.

Mr. Etheridge seemed sorry to see them go as well. I think the station must be awfully big and hollow-sounding for one man to live in alone. He said he tried one summer to have his wife, Frances, and the children come live with him. But Frances said it was too lonely out here on Pea Island.

With nobody else around but us and Mr. Etheridge only allowed to go see his family once a week or so, we figured on being good neighbors. Mr. Etheridge had his fishing skiff moored sound side, and sometimes Daddy and I went fishing with him. He also had a fenced-in garden and even a hog he was fattening up. When we found horseshoe crabs caught in our gill net, we brought them over for Mr. Etheridge's hog to eat.

With the warm weather, speckled trout and mullet were running, and our purse seine was always full. We had to check the gill net morning and evening, because if we left the fish for too long, they'd spoil in the warm sound water. We preserved them in strong brine until we could sail to Roanoke Island to sell our haul.

I helped Grandpa finish our garden fence. On one of our trips to Manteo, we bought seeds and later planted melons, collards, turnips, carrots, sweet potatoes, and tomatoes. They were sprouting up nicely in the sandy plot we'd prepared by burying fish heads there all year.

By July, the summer heat settled in like an itchy wool blanket. We stopped cooking indoors and dug a fire pit outside to use. Our fish and pan bread tasted good and smoky. In the evening, as it was getting dark, we'd open the window and door to the cabin, take a bit of brush and light it on fire, then blow out the flame and get it smoking real good. We'd bring that inside in a pot so it would fill the cabin with smoke and run out the mosquitoes and yellow flies. Between cooking outdoors and smoking out the cabin, my clothes always smelled of fire.

Grandpa was spending his time in the garden, weeding, tying up plants, picking beetles off the leaves. Some days I helped him, and in between working, he told me stories.

"Did I ever tell you how your Grandma Dahlia and I got separated?" he asked one day, his head leaning back against the garden fence where we'd sat down to rest.

I blinked. He never had told me that story. I'd always wondered but thought it would be mean-hearted to ask.

"No, Grandpa, I don't believe you have," I said.

He closed his eyes, and I felt him going back in time, remembering. "Once your daddy was born, my Dahlia used to come see me on Saturday nights with him slung to her back, sleeping. Mistress Callie let her stay overnight, then, and she and your daddy spent Sundays with me."

I tried to imagine Daddy as a little baby, and I laughed. Grandpa opened his eyes a slit, then closed them again and continued.

"Things were going along the way we thought they always would. I'd work all week, sunup to sundown, with thoughts of

Saturday night keeping me going. Then the war came. Mistress Callie's husband went off to fight the Yankees, and Dahlia said there wasn't hardly anything for her and your daddy to eat at their place anymore. I took to saving what I could from my rations to send home with them.

"About a year after the war started, two Saturdays went by and my Dahlia didn't come. I asked Master Johnson could I have a pass so I could go see what was the matter."

Grandpa's face, with the sun showing up the hollows and creases, looked sad.

"When I got to Mistress Callie's place, my Dahlia was gone. The mistress said she couldn't hardly run the farm without her husband there, and the food stores were so low she had to sell off her best hands. I wanted to kill the old woman right then—wring her neck like a scrawny chicken. But I controlled myself. Real quiet, I said, 'Then you won't want to be feeding my son,' and I went to fetch your daddy from the quarters. He was about two years old, I reckon. I carried him back to Master Johnson's place.

"Master Johnson didn't ask me a thing—I guess he figured I'd gotten him a new slave boy for free. And Mistress Callie never came looking for her stolen property either. She must have been too guilty about selling off my Dahlia like that. And she didn't want to feed a child too young to work.

"Right about that time, the war came close and all day we heard the boom-boom of guns and cannons. You could feel it in your chest—it shook the earth. And the sky turned dark with black clouds that came from all the gunpowder. Master Johnson said the Yankees would be coming soon. He wrapped up his money and silver in a sheet, then took me into the woods with him. He told me to climb up this rotten tree—it was hollow with a hole up high—and drop the sack down in. If the Yankees killed him, he said, I'd know where it was.

"Now, my kinfolk used to say that old Master Johnson was my daddy, but I never believed them until that day. My mamma died before I could ask her was it true. But he never had any white children of his own, and here he was showing me his hiding place."

"Did the Yankees come?" I asked.

"They came, all right. They didn't kill Master Johnson, but they took every stitch of meat out of our smokehouse and near emptied both the corncribs. Then they set fire to the master's house. We all ran with buckets of water to put the fire out—it would have been one sorry sight, Master Johnson having to sleep in the slave quarters after his house burned down!"

Grandpa laughed, then coughed a bit.

"Did the Yankees find the silver?" I asked.

"Lord, they tore up the place something awful looking for it, slicing the featherbeds with knives and breaking open crates and jugs. They knew he'd hid it. I think that's why they set the house afire—they were angry about not finding the money.

"A few years later, when the war ended, Master Johnson says to me, 'Ulysses, you're as free as I am now. You can stay on and work for me, and I'll make sure you have what you need, or you can leave.' I didn't stay long. When I was fixing to leave, Master Johnson took a piece of muslin and wrapped some money up in it and gave it to me. That's when I knew he was my daddy—he didn't have to do that.

"I used that money to buy our first fishing skiff. When I sold my first load of fish, I started putting ads in the newspapers for my Dahlia, so she'd know where I was and that I was looking for her. Everybody was putting ads in the papers in those days—seemed like every man and his uncle was looking for kin they'd lost."

He was quiet for a time, rocking his head back and forth gently against the wooden fence rail.

"I guess I'm the only one still putting ads in. Seems everyone else either found their kin or gave up looking."

I put my hand on his arm and squeezed. "You want a drink of water, Grandpa?"

We both got up and went to the rain barrel.

"We can put in another ad when we go with Daddy to Manteo," I said. "We've sold so many fish I'm sure he's got an extra dollar for you."

Grandpa nodded, but his eyes looked far away, like he was still seeing a North Carolina past that I would never know.

fOURTEEN

I dreamed of fire—of red flames leaping from the rescue station roof to the lookout deck. But it was Grandpa, burning up with fever next to me, who'd made me have the dream.

"Daddy, Grandpa's sick," I whispered in the darkness.

Daddy lit the fish-oil lamp. I got a cool wet rag for Grandpa's forehead, and Daddy propped him up so he could sip some water.

"How you feeling, old man?" Daddy asked.

"Just tell whoever's hitting my head with that brick to stop, and I'll be fine," Grandpa said.

"That bad?" Daddy asked. His forehead was wrinkled with worry.

Grandpa nodded slightly and eased himself back down on the bed.

"I'm taking you to Doc Fearing in the morning," Daddy said firmly.

Grandpa groaned and rolled over.

I climbed into bed with Daddy. Before he put out the lamp, I saw the fearful look in his eyes.

The next morning, Daddy said to help him get Grandpa to the skiff so we could take him to Manteo to see Doc Fearing. But Grandpa said he'd never been to a doctor in his life, and he felt too miserable to see one now. They argued for a while, and Grandpa won.

The day after that, Grandpa was feeling good enough to get out of bed, so Daddy ordered him to get in the skiff for a trip to Manteo. Grandpa said he was getting better on his own and didn't need to waste Daddy's money on some old ugly doctor. They argued until Grandpa won.

The weather was hot, and Grandpa said he wanted a bath. I went with him to the sound, where we waded in, being careful to stay away from the stinging sea nettles that floated on top of the water. When Grandpa asked me to scrub his back, I did it gently, running my hands over the raised scars that ran in jagged crisscross patters over his skin. It turned my stomach to think that the man who had made those scars, so many years ago, was also my great-grandfather.

Three days later, Grandpa got much sicker again and took to his bed, shivering and moaning that his head was about to explode, it hurt so bad. I sat with him and kept a cool rag on his forehead.

Mr. Etheridge paid us a visit. He said Grandpa looked like he had malaria, and that in a day or so, when he felt a little better, he should go see Doc Fearing to get medicine or he'd just get terrible sick again like he was now. Then he told us the story of how he'd had to do a rescue when he had malaria back in 1881.

"I would have liked to be abed, the chills and fever were so bad," he said, "but a gale blew up and the schooner *Thomas J. Lancaster* ran aground. Lord, that was a dark day. The captain must have tied his youngest daughter to the rigging, then tried to save his two other little girls who'd been washed overboard. The captain and both girls drowned. We found the youngest child, dead, hanging upside down by her feet in the rigging. The cold wind and wet must have killed her. She couldn't have been more than three years old. We did manage to save half the crew and the captain's wife, though I reckon she'd rather have died with her husband and three daughters."

I didn't think that story was a very good way to cheer up a sick person, but Grandpa looked a lot brighter by the time Mr. Etheridge left. And the best part was that he agreed to see Doc Fearing and ask for quinine, the same medicine that had made Mr. Etheridge better.

The next day was hot, with no wind, but Grandpa said he felt well enough to walk to the skiff. Daddy and I took turns rowing across the still water, the oars splashing between the weeds and sea nettles. When I wasn't rowing, I scooped up water to pour over my head to ease the heat.

In Manteo there was hardly a breeze to blow away the yellow flies and mosquitoes, and they about ate me up. We supported Grandpa, one on each side of him, to walk him to Doc Fearing's house.

As we opened the gate and started up the front walkway, Grandpa stopped. "Roses," he said in a hoarse voice.

"Come on, Grandpa, we're almost there," I said.

"Take me to those roses," he demanded.

Daddy glanced at me, then toward Doc Fearing's front windows, like he hoped these white folks wouldn't mind an old, sick colored man sniffing at their garden.

The roses were pink, bug-eaten, and wilting in the late July heat. Grandpa stumbled over to them and took a long breath of their perfume. "That's it," he said softly. "That's just the way she smelled, those Saturday nights."

I leaned over the rose blossoms, closed my eyes, and sniffed, imagining that I was hugging Grandma Dahlia and burying my nose in the nape of her neck. It was a sweet, rich smell.

The door to the house swung open, and when I opened my eyes, Mrs. Fearing was standing on the front porch with her hands on her hips.

"What on earth are you doing?" she snapped.

Daddy said Grandpa was sick and we were here to see Doc Fearing, but none of us offered an explanation as to why we were in her garden. She looked us up and down, and I realized that we must have appeared sorrowfully ragged. We wore clothes mended with my rough stitches, had sand stuck to our skin where we were sweaty, and I was half-soaked with the brackish water I'd poured over my head.

"He'll see you on the porch," she said finally, and went back inside.

Doc Fearing brought his black bag out with him. "Ulysses, you look terrible," he told Grandpa.

"I figure I must be almost dead, the way everyone keeps insisting I come see you," said Grandpa. "We should have saved ourselves a trip and gone to see the reverend instead."

The doctor laughed a little but then frowned as he pulled down Grandpa's eyelids and examined them.

"Keeper Etheridge had malaria and he got all better, right?" I asked.

Daddy put his hand on my shoulder and shushed me. "Let the doctor do his work, son," he said.

I slapped a mosquito on my leg.

"Mmm-hmmm," Doc Fearing murmured as he held Grandpa's wrist, pulled out his pocket watch, and stared at it for a while. "Your pulse is very rapid," he said. "I want you back in bed immediately."

"I told them that's where I belonged," Grandpa said.

Doc Fearing went inside and came back with a brown glass bottle and two tin cups, one full of water, the other with a little molasses and a spoon in it. Into the molasses he poured a small mound of dark powder from the glass bottle and mixed it with the spoon. He told Grandpa to take the powder three times a day for ten days.

When Grandpa spooned the medicine into his mouth, he screwed up his face like he'd just eaten cow dung, and reached quickly for the cup of water. He said if the malaria hadn't killed him in ten days, surely the taste of that powder would.

"Get him to bed, keep him comfortable, and make sure he takes the quinine powder," Doc Fearing told Daddy. Daddy promised he would.

As we rowed home, the sun sank low over the sound and turned red in the summer haze. A little breeze picked up and cooled us off. And I was glad Grandpa had gotten the medicine that would make him better.

fIfTEEN

On August 1, the life-saving crewmen came back. They all looked fattened up, from their wives' cooking, no doubt. They said George Midgett was feeling somewhat better but had failed his physical exam and wouldn't be returning. Lewis Wescott, who used to be just the winter man, came back to work in August with everyone else and took over Mr. Midgett's place of surfman number two. This December they'd need a new winter man. Secretly, I was glad that William wasn't yet old enough to fill the position.

Grandpa was feeling a little better and asked me didn't I have anything better to do than put wet rags on an old man's forehead all day. I shrugged. "If I leave, will you take your powder?" I asked him. He nodded solemnly.

I decided to walk up to the Oregon Inlet station, where the

surfmen had returned as well. The day was warm, with puffy summer clouds and waves that rolled in one at a time. I walked at the edge of the water, splashing into it when I got hot. I picked up scallop shells and threw them sidearmed at the glassy parts between the waves, trying to make them skip.

At the Oregon Inlet station, Mr. Willis was on the lookout deck. I waved to him and called hello. Mr. Forbes was in the cookhouse fixing supper, and the other surfmen were all off fishing, having finished their drills for the day. I asked Mr. Forbes for a drink, so he sat me down with a cup of water and a mound of sweet potatoes to peel and chop for him.

"I heard George Midgett won't be back this season," he said.

I was just nodding and saying, "That's right," when suddenly there was a loud thwack as something crashed against the windowpane.

"Stupid birds," Mr. Forbes mumbled. He went outside and came back in holding a limp, silky black loon. "Too bad it wasn't a duck, or I'd add it to the stew," he said.

"Loons are no good to eat?" I asked.

Mr. Forbes chuckled. "They are if you like to eat dirt."

He laid the bird down on the table and went back to chopping onions. I picked up its head and let it drop with a thump. "What are you going to do with it?" I asked.

"I'm taking a run in to Manteo to deliver and pick up the mail tomorrow. I'll bring it to my dogs," he said.

I finished my water and was about to ask for another cup when Mr. Forbes marched over to the window and peered out. "Son of a—" He glanced at me. "That rascal of a salesman is back. Two days into the active season, and he's arriving at suppertime again." He stomped back to his chopping block and stabbed his cleaving knife in so that it stood straight up. "It's enough that he comes by here on payday with tobacco and eyeglasses and anything else he can get the men to spend their money on before they can take it home to their families. But now he wants me to feed him every other day as well!" His face was red and his eyes flashed. "Quick, Nathan, fill a pot with water!"

I didn't ask why, just pulled a big stewpot down from its hook, put it in the sink, and pumped water into it as fast as I could. Mr. Forbes stuffed the vegetables we'd already chopped into a sack and shoved it in the cupboard.

Together we lifted the stewpot onto the stove, and with a sly grin, Mr. Forbes threw in one unpeeled sweet potato and the dead loon. Then he covered the pot and sat down, ready to greet our guest.

There was a knock at the door. A short, stubby white man stuck his head in. "I was passing through your neighborhood. Wanted to see if you need anything," he said cheerily. He took off his hat and wiped perspiration from his bald head. "I have an excellent new tonic, guaranteed to cure worms, prevent flatulence, and grow hair."

"Can't say that I need any of that," said Mr. Forbes. "But it's just about suppertime. You will eat with us, won't you?"

The man smiled broadly. "I was just about to say how this heat sure makes a body hungry."

Mr. Forbes got up to stir the "stew," and the salesman followed him greedily. "Went hunting this afternoon," said Mr. Forbes as he swished the unplucked loon around in the water.

The salesman stared first into the pot, then at Mr. Forbes, then at me. I kept a poker face.

"I—uh." The salesman cleared his throat. "I think I have a—uh—an engagement this evening. Yes, that's right, I have an engagement at the hotel at Nags Head."

Mr. Forbes nodded. "We won't keep you, then. You'd best sail back across the inlet before the tide goes out."

The salesman hurried out the door. When he was safely gone, Mr. Forbes and I collapsed with laughter.

As I walked home down the beach, with the evening sunlight turning gold on the waves, I smiled to myself. Tonight I could visit the men at the Pea Island station, and this time I would be the one with a story to tell. And I hoped that Grandpa would feel well enough to come listen.

SIXTEEN

Grandpa felt better for a few days, and we all figured the quinine powder had healed him up just fine. He even came out with me to pick the first melon from our garden. He balanced it on a piece of salvage board, raised up a cleaving knife and brought it down hard. The melon fell open, dripping juice onto the board.

"Look at that," Grandpa said. "Sweet as honey."

He chopped it into crescent moon slices, and we slurped the ripe fruit.

"Grandpa, I think this garden makes you almost a farmer," I said.

He grinned and wiped melon juice off his chin with the back of his hand. "It does make me happy, at any rate," he said.

He walked me along the row of tomatoes and showed me how to pinch off the sucker vines so the plant would have more

126

strength to put into making big tomatoes. He picked a fat red one and handed it to me to eat.

"Aren't we going to save anything for supper?" I asked.

"Not if you keep eating everything," he said.

We both laughed.

Two days later, the fever grabbed him again and threw him down in bed.

Daddy had fish to take to Manteo, so it was my job to stay with Grandpa. I sat with him, bringing him drinks of water, changing the cool rag on his forehead so his head wouldn't ache so much, and telling him stories. I told him about the salesman and the loon at least six times, and each time I made it more exciting. I said the salesman jumped so high in the air when he saw that loon that he nearly bumped his head on the ceiling, then he yelped like a puppy and ran out of there without even grabbing his hat. I was trying anything to help Grandpa feel better, and I think it worked, because he said, "Nathan, you're a fine story-teller."

At noon I tried to get Grandpa to eat something. He had one bite of pan bread but refused to eat any more and said he just wanted to sleep.

I tried to sit up with him while he slept, but the afternoon heat made me drowsy. The square of sunshine that filtered in through the window crept slowly from the floor to the wall as the sun moved, and a light breeze brushed my face. Finally, I crossed my arms on the side of the bed, put my head down, and fell asleep.

I don't think it was Grandpa's voice that woke me. I think it was the prickly feeling on the back of my neck, like someone's cool hand had brushed me there. Then I heard Grandpa talking.

"There you are, my love. I knew you'd come find us," he was saying, his voice soft with affection.

My eyes sprung open, and I searched the room. Grandpa had pushed the rag off his head and was propped up a little. He was looking toward the foot of the bed, his face glowing with joy. We were alone in the room.

"I'm right here, Grandpa." I touched his arm. "I didn't go anywhere."

"I know you are, boy," he said, still not looking at me but staring peacefully at a place at the foot of the bed.

I blinked, thinking I should be seeing something there, too. But there was nothing but the iron bed frame with its peeling white paint, and beyond that, Daddy's shotgun leaned up against the wall and Grandpa's hat hung on a nail. I glanced back at Grandpa. A chill of fear rattled my backbone. "Grandpa," I whispered, "what are you seeing?"

"Nathan . . ." He patted my cheek, then gave me a little shove. "Don't sit there like nobody taught you any manners. Go give your Grandma Dahlia a hug. She's come a long way to find us."

I swallowed hard and stared at Grandpa. "There's no one there," I said, shaking my head slightly.

"I knew you'd find us," Grandpa said. His voice sounded strangely weak. "Didn't you always say she would, Nathan? Well, you were right." He lay back down, the strength seeming to flow out of him like water out of a burlap sack. "I knew you'd find us," he said again, softly. "Nathan, go tell your daddy his mamma has finally come home." Then the joy on his face relaxed into blankness, and his eyes froze in a stare at the ceiling.

I jumped up. "Grandpa!" I cried. I shook him hard. His mouth dropped open, and a stream of drool oozed out the side. "Grandpa!" I screamed it and pounded on his chest. His face wouldn't change. His eyes wouldn't blink.

My hands trembled. "Grandpa, come back!" I cried. I touched his neck and felt the stillness there. No breath. No heartbeat. I let the tears run down my cheeks and drip onto his shirt.

"You promised," I whispered, "that I'd be grown before you let us bury you."

The light in the room faded with the sunset. Daddy would be at our boat mooring soon. I stood and braced myself to take him the news.

That was when it happened. As I brushed past the foot of Grandpa's bed on my way out the door, I breathed in the sweet, rich scent of roses.

SEVENTEEN

Daddy punched the mooring pole when I told him.

"I knew it," he cried. "I should have made him go that very first morning—tied him up and dragged him there if I had to." He kicked the hull of the skiff. "Oh God—I waited too long." He shut his eyes tight and pressed his fingers into his brow. "And I brought him out here to live, where there's no colored doctor. If we'd been in Elizabeth City, Doc Moore would have come to the house." His voice cracked with the pain of it, and his shoulders slumped. The strong, hard mask was gone.

"Daddy?" I said it timidly and reached out my arms.

He folded me into a hug. We both cried, dripping tears onto each other's shoulders. Mosquitoes buzzed around our heads.

After a time, Daddy straightened his back and dried his face on his sleeve. "Help me with these nets," he said. "And we've got work to do at home." We pulled the nets out of the skiff and carried them to the cabin.

It was a terrible lonely feeling, washing Grandpa's body and dressing him in his best clothes. It felt like somebody had tied an anchor weight to my chest and it was hanging there, heavy and sad. Daddy and I didn't talk much, just did what had to be done.

We gave Grandpa a Pea Island burial, the way the surfmen did when sailors died far from home. The surfmen stood with Daddy and me in a circle around Grandpa's coffin while Mr. Etheridge said a few words about Grandpa and about the afterlife. Then we buried him in the sand under a quiet stand of pines.

I left the pine grove with everyone else. Mr. Irving and Mr. Wescott had gotten together and cooked up a peach cobbler, and they invited us to the station to eat it. The surfmen all tried to distract us from being sad, with food and talk, the way folks always do at funerals. I could see in Daddy's eyes that it wasn't working very well. It wasn't working for me, either, so I slipped off to the pine grove and sat down near the mound of sand that was Grandpa's very own piece of the earth. I closed my eyes and listened to the rolling of the waves in the distance and the calling of seabirds.

"I wish you'd gotten what you wanted, Grandpa," I said. "A real farm, and Grandma Dahlia to work it with you."

A fox darted past and startled me. I scrambled to my feet, suddenly uneasy to be in the woods by myself with a corpse, even if it was only Grandpa. "I'll say what I came to say real quick, Grandpa," I said out loud. "That *somebody* in this family ought to get what they want, and William and Floyd and Daddy are all going to have a big surprise, because I *am* going to be a surfman." Then I took off running and didn't stop until I'd reached the station house.

The rest of August gave us hot, sunny days and warm, starry nights. My bed felt empty, like I was always waiting for someone to nudge me and grumble that I was taking up too much room or yank the covers just as I was getting comfortable. No one did. I wanted to tell Daddy that we had too many holes in our family now, and maybe we should move back to where we had some kin. But I didn't.

The surfmen tried to help me feel better. Mr. Etheridge showed me his logbook, and how he filled it in every day with information about the weather, surf, and wind, who was on watch during the day, and who walked the patrols at night. He showed me the duty roster, with the surfmen's names and what number position they held:

Benjamin Bowser   No. 1

Lewis Wescott   No. 2

Dorman Pugh   No. 3

Theodore Meekins   No. 4

Stanley Wise   No. 5

William Irving   No. 6

• • •

A northeaster brought in September, and the heat finally broke. On September 29, we heard over the telegraph lines from Washington, D.C., that a hurricane was headed toward the mid-Atlantic and New England coast. The hurricane missed us, but we got a storm strong enough to knock out the telephone and telegraph wires to the station. The telephone lineman came, and Daddy and the surfmen and I helped him find the breaks, testing the wires almost the whole length of the island.

On October 4, we got a wire that said a northeaster was headed our way. Mr. Meekins said this was just the beginning of the stormy season. Daddy and I bridled off our fishing skiff the way we always did before a big storm so she wouldn't be destroyed by the rising water and wind. We waded into the sound and made sure our four mooring poles were pounded in good and deep. They were in four directions out from the boat, with the boat right in the center of them. We tethered the skiff to the poles with four long ropes. That would hold her firmly, let her rise up if the water rose, and keep her from pulling too hard on any one rope.

On October 8, a storm out at sea gave us such a high, rough tide that we had to move all the station's firewood to higher ground to keep it from being washed away.

On October 9, a northeast gale started in the afternoon and blew all night. It rattled the wall boards of our cabin and made the fish-oil lamp in the kitchen swing like a ghost hand was pushing it.

On October 10, the northeaster got stronger and continued to blow all day. It made my ears ring and tired me out with its howling and shaking. Daddy and I trudged through the rain and wind to the station to get away from our own lonely cabin for a while. Mr. Etheridge said if the storm got any worse, we should come stay with them before we got blown away.

In the morning on October 11, Daddy told me to bundle up some dry clothes; we were going to stay at the Pea Island station. We put on our heavy rain slickers and rolled up our breeches. Rain blew sideways. The tide had washed clear up to our garden fence. Sea foam scuttled across our yard and caught in the brush like tufts of gray cotton. I closed my eyes against the blowing sand and felt its grit under my eyelids.

Inside the station house, we slammed shut the doors against the wind. Mr. Meekins said he'd never even seen the man from Oregon Inlet he was supposed to meet on patrol last night. "Must be the overwashing tide," he said. "They've got less of a spit of land up there—they might well be underwater by now."

The storm threw sand and rain against the shutters like handfuls of pebbles. With each gust the station shivered and swayed, and the surf, already crashing over the boat ramp, rumbled in my ears like thunder.

Mr. Etheridge canceled the evening and night patrols. There was no beach left to patrol, only rolling ocean from sea side to sound side. The lookout deck patrol would have to be enough, he said.

We opened cans of peaches for supper. No one wanted to venture through the waves to the cookhouse. As we sat eating, a loud pounding sounded on the double doors at the end of the station. I looked up. Who would be out in this raging storm?

There was a frozen moment as the surfmen looked at each other and waited. The pounding came again, water splashed in between the doors, and in an instant everyone was on their feet. "Take life preservers!" Mr. Etheridge shouted.

"Hoist the chairs!" someone else cried, and "Get those doors *open!*"

Men threw chairs onto the table, Mr. Bowser strapped a cork life jacket onto my chest, and the ocean exploded into the room. Waves of seawater rushed past my legs. A stray chair slammed against my shin, knocked me down, and I swallowed a huge gulp of salt water.

"Take the boy upstairs!" Mr. Bowser yelled.

Daddy yanked my arm and dragged me to my feet. I was coughing and spitting out salt. As he pushed me up the steps, I looked back. Another wave rolled in through the open back doors of the station house and out the open front doors. The men scurried to gather floating debris: firewood, the bellows, a footstool. They threw it all onto the "higher ground" of the table, Beaver stove, and bookshelves.

Upstairs in the dormer, Daddy slapped me on the back to help me stop choking. "You going to be all right up here?" he asked.

I nodded. He left to go help the surfmen, and I plopped down on a wooden trunk. Even though the night was warm, I shivered in my clammy clothes. I looked out the tiny porthole window at the dark, tangled sea. Lines of foam crisscrossed it in a confused jumble. And downstairs, high tide rumbled through the dining hall as if the station had been built not on dry land but in the belly of the sea itself.

The tide receded, and when the last wave had rolled through the station house, the front and back doors were finally shut against the buffeting wind and rain. I ventured back downstairs. Sand, seaweed, and shells littered the floor, and the table and other high surfaces were cluttered with everything from dishes and chairs to a white ceramic spittoon.

"I'm not sweeping until I'm sure the last of those waves has hit that door," said Mr. Wescott.

As if summoned, a rogue wave gave a rap against the back doors, squirting in more salt water. "You see?" he said, raising both eyebrows. He leaned against the table to wait.

Dorman Pugh came down from his patrol on the lookout deck and surveyed the mess. His face was drenched, and water dripped off his rain suit onto the floor. He pulled a chair off the table and sat down with a thud. "This is no northeaster," he said, wiping his face with one hand. "As sure as I'm alive, we're in the jaws of a hurricane."

The other men nodded their agreement.

"Better call Oregon Inlet," he said. "See if they're still alive."

My stomach felt suddenly hollow. The Oregon Inlet station was less protected than the Pea Island station, and it was on lower ground. If high tide had nearly washed us away . . .

Mr. Etheridge picked up the telephone receiver and gave the ring for the Oregon Inlet station: two short, one long. We all waited for them to pick up. No one did. He gave the ring again and waited. And a third time. The hollowness in my stomach grew with each silent, waiting moment. No one answered. Mr. Etheridge put the telephone receiver back on its hook.

"We don't know for sure what has happened," he said. "And we have our own work to do. Theodore, I believe you're on patrol?"

Theodore Meekins nodded, put on his rain suit, and climbed the steps to take his place on the lookout deck.

The wind seemed to scream louder, and the window shutters rattled as if the storm was clamoring to enter. I took hold of a broom and set my mind to the sweeping up of seaweed and shells. I dared not think of the Oregon Inlet crew or of where my body would be flung if the walls around me lost the battle and were exploded by the hurricane.

No one spoke as we sorted out the debris and began to put things in order. The storm was too loud to shout over, anyway.

I must have been the first to smell it. There was no mistaking it—a Coston flare has its own sharp, acrid odor. I stopped sweeping and looked toward the stairwell. By the time Theodore Meekins stumbled down the steps into the room, each of the men had caught the smell and was waiting. We all watched him, dreading what he would announce.

"God help us" was all he said.

EIGHTEEN

"Where is it?" Mr. Etheridge demanded.

"To the south, no more than two miles," Mr. Meekins replied.

"The surfboat is useless in this storm," said Mr. Etheridge. "Man the beach cart and driving cart, and hitch both mules, lame or not, or we'll never make it."

The men scrambled to don rain slickers and life preservers, and gather lanterns, blankets, and flares. I ran upstairs to get my rain slicker. One thing was clear in my mind: I was going. I would help pull the carts, I'd do whatever they asked, and I'd stay out of the way. If I was going to be a surfman, storms like this one better not scare me off. And Daddy better not try to stop me.

When Mr. Bowser saw me with my rain slicker and life preserver on, he started to shake his head. Then he thought a moment and said, "Oh hell, I'd rather have you where I can see you, anyway." He handed a life preserver to Daddy. "George, we could use your help, and there's no guarantee this place won't collapse—it might be safer outside."

We pushed out into the storm. The wind beat my ears and chest and made it hard to breathe. Rain and blowing spray stung my face. My slicker flapped like rapid gunfire.

I heard the burst of an explosion and saw a red rocket shoot into the sky. Mr. Etheridge was signaling the wrecked ship again. In answer, to the south in the distance, came a flash of red.

"Open boat room doors—man the beach cart!" Mr. Etheridge shouted over the howling wind.

Waves rolled past my legs and splashed me up to my waist. The government team was led out of their stall and hitched, one to the driving cart and the other to the beach cart. I lifted one of the drag ropes over my shoulder and, on the command of "Forward!" as the mules and surfmen pulled, I pulled.

The wind was at our backs, and gusts made me fall to my knees. The ocean was a jumble of foam and crashing waves. When the waves pushed us too hard and the currents threatened to topple all of us, we stopped to get our bearings.

The red signal came from the ship again. We were closer now, but our progress proceeded in inches. The ocean frothed white. Foam, like thick soapsuds, blew sideways across our path.

"Forward, dammit." Mr. Bowser pulled on the lead mule.

Snot ran from my nose and dripped into my mouth. Each step wearied my legs. My brain deadened until there was only the slow movement of my legs through the water and the bite of the drag rope on my shoulder.

Finally, I heard the blessed shout: "Halt!"

I stumbled forward and caught my balance on the side of the beach cart. I faced the sea and the wind. There was the sunken ship, hardly thirty yards from us. She was a mass of dark hull and white torn sails against the foaming sea, rocking on her side, her cabin and much of her starboard already demolished by the heavy surf. As I stood with my mouth open, panting, the wind blew my cheeks floppy and dried my tongue.

A cheer went up from the sailors aboard the ship. They'd spotted us and had high hopes that they would soon be rescued. I expected to hear the command "Action," to begin the breeches-buoy rescue, but heard nothing. It took me a moment to realize what Keeper Etheridge must already have figured out: our equipment was useless. There was no way to dig a hole for the sand anchor under these rolling waves, nowhere to set up the Lyle gun.

That's when I heard Mr. Meekins's voice above the din of wind and surf. "Those waves won't stop me from swimming through them—they're all blown over, hardly taller than a man," he said.

Swim? Swim out into that raging sea?

I stood rigid and watched as Mr. Etheridge pulled a large-sized shot line out of the beach cart and helped Mr. Meekins tie it around his waist. Mr. Pugh was tied in as well, and the heaving stick, attached to its own line, was secured to Mr. Meekins's body. The wind shoved at me and buffeted my ears. It was unthinkable, what these men were doing. Violence swirled around us—a deadly, churning mix of wind and sea. And these two surfmen were walking *into* it.

NINETEEN

"Man the ropes," shouted Mr. Etheridge. "One of them goes down, we'll haul them both back in."

Mr. Meekins and Mr. Pugh were dark forms against the white foam, plodding into the surf. Powerful waves smacked them in the chest. They ducked their heads down and pushed forward.

I watched with a sick feeling in my stomach as the realization crept over me: I would never be able to do what these men were doing. The words of their motto ran through my head: "You have to go out, but you don't have to come back." In that moment I knew, with not a shred of doubt, that I did not have the courage to risk my life that way. The dream, and all the months of hoping, blew away as quickly as the foam off the waves. William and Floyd and Daddy were right. I would never be a surfman.

There was no time for me to wallow in my loss. The men

were paying out the ropes, and I was a fisherman—here to help. I took hold of one of the ropes. I turned my face sideways to the wind, but still it made my eyes blurry with tears. Blindly, I let the rope out, hand over hand, then squinted out toward the ship. A ladder had been lowered, and the sailors leaned over the side, waiting. Mr. Meekins and Mr. Pugh were almost there.

I heard another cheer from the men on the ship. When I peered out, Mr. Meekins was swinging the heaving stick and line. He let it fly and it landed on deck. The sailors would tie the line to the ship so that the rope could help steady the surfmen as they made their way from ship to shore and back again.

Soon we were hauling rope back in. The surfmen would be carrying one of the sailors between them now. I squinted into the spray. Where was the rescued sailor? Mr. Meekins and Mr. Pugh were on their way back, but without a third man between them. Mr. Meekins was carrying something a little larger than a Lyle gun.

What in the world could be more important to save off that ship than the lives of the men on board? I shook my head and hauled rope. The surfmen were half walking, half swimming, pushing forward, the waves smacking against their backs and seeming to want to spit them out of the sea.

As the surfmen drew closer, I heard what sounded like the squalling of an alley cat. Mr. Meekins handed over his bundle and shouted, "Get it into dry blankets before it goes blue!" The bundle was passed from man to man, until it was handed to me and I found myself looking into the terrified eyes of a screaming child.

Daddy put his arm around my shoulders. "The driving cart," he shouted over the din of waves and wind. In the driving cart, which was nothing more than an open wagon, dry blankets were packed under oilskins.

We crouched next to the cart, and it gave us some protection from the storm. The child clung to my neck. He was drenched and shivering miserably. I tried to loosen his grip so I could get his wet clothes off, but he just clung tighter. He was crying more softly now. "Mamma?" he whimpered.

I gave Daddy a pleading look. What if his mother had already been washed overboard and drowned? Daddy stood, cupped his hands around his eyes, and looked in the direction of the ship. "They're carrying a woman back now," he said.

"Your mamma is coming," I told the child. He looked to be about three or four years old, with pale white skin and a shock of thick brown hair. "Let's get you warm before she gets here."

We had the boy wrapped in a dry blanket by the time his mother came running to him, cried, "Thomas!" and clutched him to her own wet clothing with such passion that she probably got him half drenched again.

The lady, who told us her name was Mrs. Gardiner, said she'd be warm enough in her wet dress under blankets and oilskins. No sooner had we settled her with Thomas than we heard the cry "Ho, this man is injured!"

I ran to see. A young sailor had just been delivered by the surfmen. Blood dripped from his head and stained his life preserver. His lips were a sickly blue. He took two steps, then collapsed face first into the shallow water. Mr. Bowser dragged him up by his armpits and pulled him toward the driving cart.

"George, take over my place with the ropes," he shouted to Daddy. "Nathan, come help me."

The sailor looked hardly older than me, with dirty blond hair that had a bloody gash the size of a pole bean running through it.

"Treat the bleeding first, then the hypothermia," I said as I recalled the words from the medical books and they comforted me with their matter-of-factness.

Mr. Bowser grunted as we lifted the sailor into the driving cart. "You did study well, Nathan," he said.

Mr. Bowser sent me for the medicine chest, then I held a compress against the man's head wound while Mr. Bowser began to remove his wet clothes. That's when Mr. Bowser seemed to notice Mrs. Gardiner for the first time.

"Ma'am, we're going to have to . . ." He cleared his throat. "The boy's hypothermic, so his wet clothes have to . . ."

Mrs. Gardiner rolled her eyes in annoyance. "Oh, for heaven's sake!" she exclaimed. She immediately went to work to pull off the man's boots, help Mr. Bowser get the rest of his clothes off, and bundle him in a dry blanket.

"Are there any other injured on board?" Mr. Bowser asked as he wrapped a bandage around the man's head.

"No, only Arthur," she said. "He took quite a fall when the ship ran aground."

Arthur groaned and his eyes fluttered open. "Lord, I'm cold," he complained.

Suddenly there was a commotion at the ropes. "Heave!" Mr. Etheridge shouted. "Haul them all in!"

"They've lost their footing!" I cried.

Mr. Bowser grasped me by the arms. "Take over here. I'm sure you know what to do." Then he ran to help with the ropes.

My hands felt clammy and shaky, but once again the words from the books came back to steady me: "Rub the legs and arms with linseed oil until warmth returns. . . ." I rummaged in the medicine chest, found the linseed oil, and poured some into my palm.

"This will warm you, sir," I said loudly enough to be heard over the wind.

Arthur nodded his bandaged head and watched nervously as I rubbed the oil into his feet and calves, then his hands and arms. He gave Mrs. Gardiner a quizzical look. "Ain't he young to be a doctor?" he asked her.

She patted his shoulder and smoothed the hair off his forehead. "He seems to know what to do, dear," she said.

"I am warming up," he said.

I lifted the lantern to look at Arthur's face and saw that his lips were no longer blue.

Just then a tall white man appeared, dressed in a captain's coat, his long hair flying in the wind. He reached up into the driving cart and pulled Mrs. Gardiner to him, pressing his cheek against hers. He must have asked about Thomas, because she pointed to him, bundled and sleeping in the cart. "My God, they've saved the whole crew!" he cried. He looked around at me and Arthur, and at the other rescued sailors and the surfmen who were now gathering around the driving cart in preparation for the long trip back through the storm to the station.

"My good men," he said, his voice shaking, "we owe you our lives."

TWENTY

The trek back to the station took every ounce of strength any of us had. Mrs. Gardiner, Thomas, and Arthur rode in the driving cart. The rest of us shouldered the drag ropes and pressed our bodies against the raging wind as if it were a solid wall of force. It thundered in my ears, lashed my face, beat me to my knees more times than I could count. The two-mile trudge felt like two hundred.

No one wanted food when we got there—just dry clothes from the box donated by the Women's National Relief Association and a cot to fall asleep on. Mr. Irving stumbled wearily up the steps to the lookout deck to keep watch. Mr. Etheridge gave his room to Captain Gardiner and his family and slept in the dormer with us.

It was late morning before anyone stirred. The storm outside had died down some, though I could still hear rain hitting the side of the station in sheets.

Mr. Wescott jostled my foot. "Come help me cook, Nathan," he said. "These folks will be powerful hungry when they wake up."

Downstairs, Mr. Etheridge was at his desk writing the wreck report for the E. S. *Newman*.

"Did you call Oregon Inlet?" Mr. Wescott asked.

"The phone lines are down. After we eat, I'll send someone to see what happened up there," said Mr. Etheridge.

In the cookhouse, as I sliced bacon, I felt small and insignificant. Yesterday, and for months now, I'd been a surfman in training. It had made me feel a little taller, a little more like a man. It had made me feel like I was climbing up to a higher place. But this morning, sitting in the cookhouse with a carving knife and a slab of bacon, I felt unimportant. I was just a helper—nothing more.

A pounding on the cookhouse door brought me back from my thoughts. Mr. Davis of the Oregon Inlet crew pushed open the door.

"You're alive then, are you?" Mr. Wescott clapped him on the back as he came in.

"Barely that," said Mr. Davis. "That storm nearly killed us three or four times. And the station is half wrecked—wall boards blown out, boat ramp gone, and the flagpole, key post box, bulkhead—all that's gone. The cookhouse and smokehouse are full of sand. They need to move that station in a hurry, because it did us no good last night once the waves started washing through it chest high."

"What did you do?" I asked, aghast.

"First we tethered the surfboat to the leeward of the station and huddled in the boat, thinking it was safer than inside. But after four or five waves washed right in over us and almost swamped us, we cut the tethers and made for some sand hills about five hundred yards to the southwest—they were the only bit of land sticking up out of the tide."

I noticed that Mr. Davis's eyes were sunken and dark, like he hadn't slept all night. "Did you make it to the hills?" I asked.

"Had to row like madmen to keep from getting washed right past them and out into the open sea." He shuddered, remembering. "We beached the surfboat, then climbed out and lay low in the brush. Lord, that wind was strong enough to throw a man from here to Raleigh!"

The Oregon Inlet crew joined us for breakfast, since their station was in such rough shape. Around the table, stories about the night before mixed with a discussion of how those officials in Washington had better agree to move both the Oregon Inlet and the Pea Island stations to higher ground before one big storm sent both crews to their deaths.

"The island keeps moving, so we'd better keep moving with it," said the Oregon Inlet keeper.

Captain Gardiner and his sailors couldn't thank the Pea Island crew enough for what they'd done. "I had prepared to die," Captain Gardiner said. "Then I looked out, and there you were, swimming out to the ship!" He bounced Thomas on his knee, and Mrs. Gardiner sat beside him, looking small in a Women's National Relief Association dress that was several sizes too big for her.

The more we heard about the damage done to the Oregon Inlet station, the more Daddy and I realized that our homestead might need major repairs. After breakfast, we decided to go have a look.

The day was dark, warm, and humid, with a strong northwest wind and spattering rain. The island was changed. Brush had been torn up by the overwashing tide, and tree limbs had been snapped by the wind. Wooden planks—either from the *E. S. Newman* or from one of the stations—lay tangled in toppled cedar trees. We stepped over the mess, trying to find our usual path to our homestead.

It seemed to be taking a long time for us to reach our cabin. Then, with a chill, I realized we'd already walked plenty far enough. Daddy put his hand on my shoulder, and I slumped against him. "It's all gone, isn't it," I said. He drew me close, and we stood there like that, looking over the brambles and weeds, with not even a mound left to show where our cabin used to be.

Suddenly I jerked from Daddy's embrace. "The skiff!" I cried.

I ran, high-stepping over the debris, toward the marsh and the sound. If the skiff was gone, we'd have lost everything. If the skiff was gone, Daddy and I would have to work as day laborers. . . .

I gasped with relief when I saw her bobbing in the waves, pulling at the ropes slightly. I splashed right into the water to inspect the hull. Amazingly, there was only a little damage—the starboard was stove in, most likely bashed by floating debris. It wasn't bad and would be easy to repair.

Daddy splashed into the water beside me.

"She's okay," I said. "The long mooring ropes worked."

"Thank God," he said.

Standing at the edge of the marsh, Daddy put his arms around me, and I cried—with sadness over everything we'd lost, and relief about what we still had.

TWENTY~ONE

We could rebuild, Daddy said. The surfmen offered to let us stay at the station at least until we could get the cabin raised. Then we'd have to work on the smokehouse and privy and garden fence. Or we could stay with Mamma's cousins through the winter and rebuild in the spring.

It all felt confusing, and jumbled as waves in a storm. I was relieved when Daddy said, "First things first," and we concentrated on helping the surfmen and sailors with repairs to the station houses and gathering the wreckage from the *E. S. Newman*. I was even more relieved when he said we needed to spend a day fishing, then sell our haul and buy provisions so we could contribute to all the food we were eating at the station.

The wind was light northwest, the day sunny and summery,

and out on the Pamlico Sound in the fishing skiff with Daddy felt like the place I most wanted to be. We lowered our nets and hoped for them to fill with the stripers, bluefish, and puppy drum that were running this time of year.

"We'll bring the haul in fresh today," said Daddy.

"All right," I said. A visit to Roanoke Island would do my spirit good.

We didn't say much, just enjoyed the calm quiet of each other's company. The light wind and sunshine, after so many days of storm, were a welcome pleasure.

If this was to be my life—fishing day after day—then I should find the enjoyment in it: the appreciation of sunny, warm days out on the sparkling water; the satisfaction of pulling in a heavy net; the friendly visits to Roanoke Island to sell the day's catch and meet old friends.

But still I wondered about what Grandpa had said—how if you work real hard, you can get your dreams even though they might not look the way you imagined they would, like the way he got the skiff to work in for himself with Daddy and me, instead of the farm to work on for himself with Grandma Dahlia. Certainly, fishing wasn't my surfman dream in different clothing. I had wanted to do something big, something great. I'd wanted to fight battles and win. I'd wanted to help people, to save people's lives. And I'd wanted to push myself into a bigger dream than the one Daddy had dreamed up for me. I watched the fat, puffy clouds drift across the sky and wondered if the way it worked for Grandpa just wasn't going to work for me.

By afternoon, we had a respectable catch and headed to Roanoke Island to sell it. We docked at Manteo, and I helped Daddy unload the fish barrels.

"Nathan! Mr. Williams!"

I turned to see Fannie running down to the dock, her black braids flying. She arrived at our boat breathless.

"We *heard*," she panted, "about the rescue, the storm . . . your cabin. I'm so sorry."

"How did you fare here?" Daddy asked her.

"There are trees down, parts of roofs torn off, and a few privies and sheds blown away. But nobody dead except Mr. Brothers's hog who got killed when the barn caved in," she answered.

"That's good," said Daddy. "Nathan, help me get this fish up to Griffin's store, then you can visit with Fannie."

Fannie and I both helped. Then we strolled back to the dock and sat on the wooden planks with our feet dangling in the water.

She asked me about the rescue, what I had done to help, and if I was scared. I answered her honestly, that those surfmen were braver than I would ever be and that I was glad to just handle the ropes and help get Arthur and little Thomas warmed up and settled. She wanted to hear about Arthur's head wound and made a scrunched-up face when I told her about the blood.

When I was done with the story, I wanted to tell her how I'd given up my dream, how I'd decided to settle for the dull, peaceful life of a fisherman. But I had never told her that I'd had the dream in the first place, so there was no reason to tell her now about it being lost. I sighed. "So now I'm back to fishing—no more excitement," I said.

"But just for a little while," she said.

I gave her a sideways look. What did she mean?

She was gazing out across the bay, swinging her legs and making the water swish between her feet. "Then you'll have to go away for a while—someplace far away, I suppose." She turned to me and smiled. "But then you'll come back."

"Fannie, what—"

She interrupted me and kept talking. "I already told my mamma what you're going to do, and she's real happy about it. And just last night, I told my Uncle Brewster—because he's been real sick, only he still doesn't think it's time yet to go to Doc Fearing—I told him soon folks won't have to be wondering if they're sick enough to call on Doc Fearing. I said because when Nathan becomes a doctor, he'll come back here, and then we'll have our own colored doctor just like they do in Elizabeth City."

My mouth dropped open, and I blinked at her. "And is there anything *else* you've got all figured out for me?" I asked, annoyed.

Fannie's eyes sparkled, and she gave me a coy smile.

I held up my hand. "Never mind," I said quickly, to keep her from answering. I scowled at her, crossed my arms over my chest, then stared out across Shallowbag Bay, thinking.

• • •

Daddy says he's glad to be back among friends and Mamma's kinfolk here on Roanoke Island. He says in a way he's glad the storm wrecked our cabin. And Miss Ella Midgett, my teacher, says she can hardly tell I've been away from schooling for a whole year — that I'm reading even better than when I left. Doc Fearing says that's good news because there's loads of reading to be done in medical school. I just got the letter from Leonard Medical School in Raleigh saying yes, if I pass the entrance examination, they'll be glad to have me as a student when I'm old enough to go. Tuition is a hundred dollars a year.

When Daddy read the letter, he took an empty jar down off the shelf and put a dollar in it. He said we'll do that every other week, even if it means freezing our toes in winter because we put a dollar in the jar instead of buying coal, and when the time comes for me to go to Raleigh, the money will be there.

AUTHOR'S NOTE

It was February 1997, and my husband, Jim, called me from Puerto Rico.

"I've got the story for your next book!" he announced.

Jim had gone to Puerto Rico to windsurf with a group of folks from the Outer Banks of North Carolina. Among the group were Ron and Kathy Pettit, who now own and live in the old Pea Island Life-Saving Station. Ron and Kathy had just been involved in a very exciting medal ceremony.

This ceremony involved the awarding of the Gold Life-Saving Medal—the highest honor in the United States Life-Saving Service—to a group of men who had long been dead. These men, the keeper and crew of the Pea Island Life-Saving Station, were being honored one hundred years after they had performed a rescue so heroic—and at so great a risk to their own lives—that they fully deserved the Gold Life-Saving Medal.

During a hurricane on October 11, 1896, when the *E. S. Newman* ran aground on a shoal off Cape Hatteras, the crew of the Pea Island Life-Saving Station came to her aid. Because their normal rescue equipment had become useless in the severe storm and overwashing tide, they improvised, tying two surfmen together with a heavy shot line and sending them out to the *E. S. Newman* to carry back one survivor at a time. They rescued everyone on board. This was the kind of courage and self-sacrifice for which white surfmen of the day received recognition. But the African-American Pea Island crew was unjustly overlooked for United States Life-Saving Service honors.

In the fall of 1993, two graduate students, David Wright and David Zoby, came across the first clues that there was an untold story lurking among the files of the United States Life-Saving Service. Little by little, they unraveled the mystery, piecing together the facts from station logs, wreck reports, letters, and other documents. By 1994, they had amassed a body of evidence that verified the fact that Keeper Richard Etheridge and his crew truly deserved the Gold Life-Saving Medal. They set about to bring the facts to the attention of the Coast Guard, which is the successor to the United States Life-Saving Service.

Wright and Zoby wrote a sixty-nine-page document detailing the facts surrounding the *E. S. Newman* rescue and asking for the Gold Life-Saving Medal to be awarded posthumously to the Pea Island crew. The document was brought to the attention of the Medals and Awards Panel of the Coast Guard by Commander Steve Rochon. A fourteen-year-old student, Kate Burkhart, wrote letters concerning the award to President Clinton and Senator Jesse Helms. People in high places listened to these four crusaders, and the result was a medal ceremony where, amid tears and applause, the racial wrongs of a hundred years ago took a step toward being righted. The Gold Life-Saving Medal came one hundred years late but was deeply appreciated by the descendants of the surfmen in attendance at the ceremony, many of whom had served or are still serving in the U.S. Coast Guard.

Readers often ask me which parts of my books are true and which parts are fiction. In *Storm Warriors*, each of the wrecks and rescues—the dates of the wrecks, the names of the vessels, the ways the rescues were done, the weather during the rescue—are true. All of the surfmen and sailors bear their real names. All of the stories told by surfmen and sailors are true stories. And yes, I have seen the photograph of Captain Squires's disembodied head and shoulders floating in the rigging of the wrecked *Louis V. Place*. I don't think it's a ghost. I think it's a double exposure—a trick done by the photographer, which apparently made good wages for the sailor who went door to door selling the photos!

During the years I researched and wrote this book, I spent many weeks living on the Outer Banks. I researched at the history centers and libraries, spent time interviewing local residents and historians, and sometimes simply walked the beach or waded in the Pamlico Sound to get a feel for the place. This all helped me re-create what life was like in Elizabeth City, on Roanoke Island, on Pea Island, and in the United States Life-Saving Service in the late 1800s.

Nathan, his father, and his grandfather, on the other hand, are fictitious characters. At first, I didn't know how I was going to place my young protagonist on Pea Island. The historical map of the area I had gotten at the National Archives made it clear that there was no town on Pea Island where Nathan and his family could live. Then one day I was at the Outer Banks History Center listening to the oral-history tapes made by Wright and Zoby in which they interviewed some of the oldest family members of the life-saving crews. On one particular tape, they were talking with Mrs. Pinky Berry, whose husband, Maxie Berry, had served in the Coast Guard on Pea Island. She was talking about the 1920s, saying that she had stayed in a little cottage near the station house. David Wright asked her, "Did your husband build the cottage for you?" Mrs. Berry said, "No. It was already there. The fishermen used it." Aha! I thought. That's it. That's Nathan's house.

I also like to use reenactment to help me better understand my stories. On one of my trips to the Outer Banks, in April, I thought I was safe in telling my friends that what I really needed

for my research was a good hurricane. April is not hurricane season. The first week and a half of our stay was pleasant, but toward
the end of the second week, a northeaster came in with 55-mph
winds, drenching rain, blowing sand, and trees bent sideways
until they looked like they'd snap. It was *perfect* for my research.
For three days, I either sat inside our shuddering cottage listening to the rattling and clattering as the storm seemed to try to
tear the walls down or bundled myself up to push out onto the
beach in the strongest wind I'd ever experienced in my life. Sand
blew into my eyes, foam scuttled across my path, and my jacket
flapped like rapid machine-gun fire around my body. I would go
out onto the beach for as long as I could stand it, feeling the force
of the wind, taking in all of the sensations. Then I'd trudge back
to the cottage and write it all down. I did this over and over again
until I had pages of description of what it was like to struggle
against a raging storm. These were the closest conditions to the
night of October 11, 1896, I could have experienced without
being evacuated from the Outer Banks.

On another trip I went out at night and walked along the
lonely, dark beach, thinking, *I am Benjamin Bowser, and I am
walking the nine-*P.M.*-to-midnight patrol.* I scanned the ocean for
wounded ships, willing myself to understand what it must have
been like to walk this beat.

I also spent many days sailing on the Pamlico Sound the
way Nathan and his father and grandfather did. Of course,

they were in their fishing skiff and I was on my windsurfer, but it's still the same *slap-slap-slap* over glistening water on a sunny, southwest day.

Although Nathan is a fictitious character, he is typical of the type of student who attended Leonard Medical School: young black men from humble circumstances who were inspired students. Many of these young men did as I suspect Nathan would do: return to the poor, rural areas they came from and provide affordable medical care to their communities.

These days, the shores of Pea Island look similar to the way they looked over a hundred years ago. It has been designated a National Wildlife Refuge, so there are still no towns or beach houses. However, New Inlet has closed up, so Pea Island is no longer an island—it is now connected to the rest of Cape Hatteras National Seashore.

The Pea Island station was rebuilt and later moved over to the sound side in Salvo, a few miles south of its original location. The fisherman's cottage, the ruins of Jesse Etheridge's house, and the hunting cabins are all gone. The Oregon Inlet Station was rebuilt and still sits near Oregon Inlet.

As you drive down Highway 12 on Pea Island, about six miles south of Oregon Inlet, you'll find a kiosk exhibit honoring the Pea Island Life-Savers. If you walk north from there along the beach, you might be able to find the ruins of the foundation of the old Pea Island Station. On Roanoke Island at the North Carolina Aquarium, you'll find on display the Gold Life-Saving Medal that was awarded to the valiant Pea Island crew.

The Chicamacomico Life-Saving Station in Rodanthe on the Outer Banks has been restored and may be visited during museum hours. Here you can see the equipment that was used by the lifesavers: the Lyle gun, the surfboat, the hawser line, and the beach cart. Reenactors even do a real breeches-buoy drill! In the Chicamacomico boathouse are reminders of the rescues performed by various Outer Banks lifesavers, including the Pea Island crew: the old wooden name plaques from the wrecked ships. In a quiet, dusty corner you can find it, as I did: the name plaque from the *E. S. Newman*.

• • •

I would highly recommend these books for further reading about the United States Life-Saving Service and the Outer Banks of North Carolina:

Mobley, Joe A. *Ship Ashore! The U.S. Lifesavers of Coastal North Carolina*. North Carolina Division of Cultural Resources, 1994.

Shanks, Ralph C., and Wick York. *The U.S. Life-Saving Service: Heroes, Rescues and Architecture of the Early Coast Guard*. Edited by Lisa Woo Shanks. Costaño Books, 1996.

Stick, David. *Graveyard of the Atlantic: Shipwrecks of the North Carolina Coast*. The University of North Carolina Press, 1952.

Wright, David, and David Zoby. *Fire on the Beach: The Untold Story of Richard Etheridge and the Pea Island Lifesavers*. Scribner, 2001.

ACKNOWLEDGMENTS

There are many people who helped me with the process of re-creating what life was like on Pea Island, Roanoke Island, and within the United States Life-Saving Service in 1896. Each individual was part of creating the whole picture, and I am extremely grateful for each person's input. First, I would like to thank David Wright and David Zoby, the men who spearheaded the research of uncovering the story of the Pea Island Life Savers. The oral-history taped interviews and written documents that they donated to the Outer Banks History Center got me started with my own research. They also acted as mentors as I wrote, answering many questions. David Wright carefully reviewed the manuscript.

Wynne Dough of the Outer Banks History Center in Manteo, North Carolina, himself a descendant of USLSS members, was an invaluable resource for information, along with Sarah Downing and the other research assistants at the center. I am also grateful to the research assistants at the Library of Congress in Washington, D.C., the National Archives in Washington D.C., the National Archives II in College Park, Maryland, and the Dare County Library in Manteo, North Carolina.

I would like to thank the many people whom I interviewed

and who guided me to information I needed: Lt. JG Tara Pettit of the Coast Guard; Outer Banks historian David Stick; Richard Darcey, Michael Halminski, and Robert Huggett of the Chicamacomico Historical Association; Ralph Shanks and James Claflin of the U.S. Life-Saving Service Heritage Association; Joe Mobley of the North Carolina Division of Archives and History; Gary Fulton of the National Archives in East Point, Georgia; Dorothy Meekins; Duke Meekins; Danny Couch; C. Barton Decker; Rudy Gray; Anthony Cohen; Mike Mangino; Lynn Murray; and Ron and Kathy Pettit.

Many thanks to my editor, Tracy Gates, who had the wisdom to tell me to go to the Outer Banks without my research materials, which resulted in a much better second draft. And many thanks to my family members, who gave editorial and emotional support: my daughter, Rachel; my father, Dad; and my husband, Jim.